THE TUTANKHAMUN MURDER

An addictive crime mystery full of twists

ROY LEWIS

Eric Ward Mystery Book 16

JOFFE BOOKS

Revised edition 2021
Joffe Books, London
www.joffebooks.com

First published in Great Britain in 2008

**Join our mailing list and become one of thousands of
readers enjoying free Kindle crime thriller, detective,
mystery, and romance books and new releases.
Receive your first bargain book this month!**

www.joffebooks.com/contact

We love to hear from our readers! Please email any
feedback you have to: feedback@joffebooks.com

ISBN: 978-1-78931-708-4

PROLOGUE

1923

The bastard was keeping him waiting, of course. Deliberately.

A typical civil-service trick, Howard Carter thought angrily. He was being kept waiting by a small, pompous, self-opinionated man seeking to inflate his own feeling of self-worth. From outside the building, across the courtyard beyond the Embassy gardens he could hear the rattle of a cart in the sweltering heat. Here in the anteroom it was cooler but he could feel the sweat gathering in the small of his back, staining his shirt. Above his head the ceiling fan circulated rhythmically, sending out a regular *thunk, thunk, thunk* sound. He shifted in his seat, feeling the anger in his chest thicken, knotting like a red-hot ball as he glared at the clerk seated behind the desk at the other side of the room.

The minor official, neatly dressed in a collar and tie, was young and smooth-cheeked, fair hair carefully parted, spectacles perched on the end of his nose and seemingly impervious to the heat. A minion; but a Cerberus, nevertheless. As the anger began to rise in Carter's throat, the clerk, perhaps sensing the frustration that gripped his guest, raised his head, smiled. 'I'm sure Sir Leonard will see you soon . . .'

From the street outside came the subdued hum of the Cairo traffic, muffled by the expanse of garden at the Embassy. Carter had always hated this place, because of its shibboleths, its airy dismissal of the realities of the outside Egyptian world, its stuffy, self-important officials, but most of all because of its refusal to support his cause, with its careful kow-towing to Egyptian sensibilities in the face of wholesale corruption and mendacity.

He leant his head back against the wall, brushed the back of his hand against his small, neatly trimmed moustache. Carter closed his eyes, controlling the anger in his chest, preparing himself for the meeting to come, but at the same time allowing his thoughts to drift back to those moments last December which he knew would continue to be the self-defining moments of his life . . .

He recalled the absolute, riveting silence that had greeted him when he went down to the site that day, the first excitement that had thundered in his veins when he heard how the boy had raised the alarm, and then the men had shown him the first step, outlined there in the dust. They had worked furiously clearing away the sand, and the steps led downward, through the hidden centuries, until finally he had found the broken shards in the entrance, the scattered pottery, and there on the door, the familiar motif that had appeared on many tombs in the valley, the jackal in triumph above the nine bound captives. The motif of the necropolis of the Valley of the Kings.

He recalled now how his hands had been trembling as he brushed away the dust and rubble from the base of the door. There were more broken shards of pottery: he could make out the cartouches stamped upon the clay: *Smenkhka-Re*, the seal of the pharaoh, and saw what he knew was the doorway to the tomb. The blood had hammered in his throat when he realised that the seals on the door itself were unbroken.

He had never been a man in complete control of himself, but he held on to his excitement then, as he held on to the simmering anger now. Immediately he was certain he had discovered a tomb he had wired his friend, benefactor, and patron, the fifth earl, Lord Carnarvon, at home in England.

* * *

'At last have made wonderful discovery in Valley; a magnificent tomb with seals intact; recovered same for your arrival; congratulations.'

After an initial hesitation — there had been so many false alarms in the past — Earl Carnarvon had replied that he would be coming out from England to the Valley of the Kings post-haste. They had both known this was their last chance after years of endeavour in the sand of the valley; the money had run out, it was to be the last year of digging. But they had succeeded at last. And succeeded beyond dreams, beyond all realistic expectations.

Carter had boarded the felucca and drifted along the broadening flow of the Nile to spend a few days preparing for the visit of his patron, making plans for the next few months' work. When the train had come lumbering into the station at Luxor he had been there on the crowded platform to meet them as they alighted. The provincial governor had been at his side, of course: news of the discovery had inevitably leaked out even though no one knew for certain what really lay under the rubble the workmen had replaced on the steps. Lord Carnarvon had come forward, whitesuited, limping and leaning on his stick with his free hand outstretched, neatly attired as always, his lean features excited, smiling. Behind him had come his daughter, his devoted companion in all his Egyptian work, Lady Evelyn: young, happy, enthusiastic. Evelyn . . .

Carter was aware of the difficulties: she was not yet twenty and he was years older than she, they were of a different social station, and yet he felt he held a special place in her heart. He was convinced that it had not been merely girlish flirtation that caused her to hold his hand, kiss his cheek when they had proceeded to the Valley of the Kings and he had first taken them to the tomb. When the excavation party had been photographed at the top of the cleared steps on the day of the official opening, her father had stood on his left but Evelyn had chosen to stand on Carter's right, linking her arm through his, pressing close to his side. Now, musing in the anteroom at the Embassy, he almost felt he could still sense the pressure of her hand on his arm . . .

And it was she who had been first to enter the tomb itself.

* * *

They had cut the hole in the upper left-hand corner of the wall and pulled out the ancient masonry. He had inserted a lit candle into the aperture as a precaution against foul gases, and then, after widening the hole a little further, had peered inside. Lord Carnarvon, Lady Evelyn and Pecky Callender had been standing behind him but Carter was barely conscious of their presence. What he saw inside the tomb had struck him dumb. The hot, fetid air inside the antechamber caused the candle flame to waver and dance and it took a little while for his eyes to become accustomed to the gloom. But at last details began to emerge in the leaping, flickering light: strange animals, the glint of gold . . . everywhere the glint of gold.

Leaning on his stick behind Carter, unable to stand the suspense, Lord Carnarvon had broken the silence. 'Can you see anything?'

He struggled to get out the answer. 'Yes . . . It's wonderful . . .'

He had stepped back then, inserted the electric torch, and each of the small party had taken the opportunity to peer into the chamber that had been closed three thousand years earlier. They were all awestruck in turn, shaken by what they had seen. Then, as the day faded, Lady Evelyn and Lord Carnarvon had returned up the steps to the entrance, and Carter and Callender finally resealed the small aperture in the wall. They climbed the steps thoughtfully, locked the wooden grille that had been placed outside the first doorway, and the small group then rode home, down the silent, moonlit Valley.

They all knew what was required of them by the Egyptian government, but that evening, after a subdued dinner at the small house where Carter had established himself near the diggings, Carter had first blurted out the suggestion. They had sat there, stared at each other, uncertain, but filled with a nervous excitement. The terms of the concession granted to Lord Carnarvon by the Department of Antiquities were explicit: in the event of any discovery at their excavations, entrance was to be undertaken only under the supervision of department officials. But Carter had endured months, years of petty officialdom and meddling from Pierre Lacau, the Director General, along with others; but it was their discovery, not Egypt's. Carnarvon's money, Carter's own expertise built up over decades, and six years of hard work had led to the unlocking of the tomb . . .

That night after dinner they rode back into the moonlit Valley, silent, each preoccupied with the enormity of what they were about to do as the looming cliffs gleamed pale about them under the bright stars and the sharp, clear moonlit sky. If the truth ever got out, there would be scandal, a reputation destroyed. But the small group — Carter, Lord Carnarvon, Lady Evelyn and Callender — rode on, unable to resist the temptation, each aware of the rising excitement in throat and chest, the longing to consummate the burning desires that now consumed them.

They dismissed the guard, unlocked the padlocked gate, descended into the corridor, reached the doorway in the wall. With Callender's assistance Carter had cut a second hole, making a breach low down as Lord Carnarvon and Lady Evelyn stood by. Then they had paused, looked at each other in the harsh light of the hand-held electric torchlight, powered by a cable run down from the tomb of Rameses VI above. It was a pause, a last uncertainty, and it held them in silence. It was broken by the young woman.

'I *must* look,' Lady Evelyn had squealed, and it was enough.

With difficulty, she wriggled through the hole they had made, and he had passed through to her the flashlight they had brought with them to the tomb.

'What can you see?' Carter had asked, unable to contain his impatience.

'As you already said,' she cried out. 'Things of wonder!'

They hesitated only a moment longer. Seized by a burning excitement Carter and Callender tore at the wall, enlarging the hole until Lord Carnarvon was able to force his body through the aperture, joining his excited daughter in the anteroom beyond. A short while later Carter stood beside them inside the chamber, while Pecky Callender, too big and heavy to force his way through the aperture, stood guard outside. Callender passed through to them the brighter hand-held light, and they could see that they were in a slender corridor, but Carter knew that the shimmering gold ahead of them would be one side of an enormous gilded shrine . . .

* * *

The ceiling fan went *thunk, thunk, thunk* in the otherwise silent Embassy office but Carter was hardly aware of the sound. He recalled the images that had been presented to them on that first incursion and how they had later learnt that the great tabernacle beyond contained a nest of smaller shrines protecting the royal sarcophagus; in one of the gilded mummiform coffins within lay the intact remains of the Pharaoh Tutankhamun. But the moments after their illicit entry remained burnt into his memory: the electric light swept its glare over walls covered in gold inlaid with blue faience, played over hieroglyphic inscriptions and symbols of protection and, when they had slid back the bronze lock bolt to enable them to open the hinged doors, they saw scattered on the floor, undisturbed in the dust of thousands of years, many beautiful objects, gold boxes, staves, alabaster vases, beautifully carved chairs, a confusion of overturned chariots, gilded statuettes, alabaster urns, clay jars and eleven sacred paddles laid out in a line, ready for the pharaoh's journey to the underworld.

Evelyn had grabbed at his hand, squeezed it, and her voice was thick with excitement. 'I told you! Wonderful things! Look at the murals!'

Pharaoh, in his guise of Osiris, Lord of the Underworld; pharaoh standing before his successor dressed as the god Horus in the blue crown and leopard skin of a *sem*-priest; Tutankhamun again as a living monarch wearing the *nemes*-headdress, holding a mace and stave. They stared at the scenes around them, murmuring their wonder; they marvelled at the workmanship, but it was in the northeast corner that they finally discovered the storeroom and found themselves facing the great gilded shrine.

Evelyn's voice was low, almost strangled. 'It's the most beautiful monument I've ever seen.'

Gilded statuettes surrounded them, gilt couches carved in the forms of animals, Anubis in his jackal-form, boxes and chests, *ushabtis*, necklaces and rings, sceptres, robes, faience cups, toys . . .

Time slipped away from them. As Callender stayed impatiently outside, guarding the entrance, the hours passed by. The entrants to the tomb were hungry for knowledge, drunk with excitement, overwhelmed by wonder, but the hot air was thick, the rising dust clogging their nostrils, lining their throats drily until finally they could take no more. But there was one last moment when they stood there, the three of them, and a tension had arisen, an unspoken desire circling about them, almost a hunger.

'Daddy . . .' Lady Evelyn pleaded.

There was a long, pregnant silence.

'We can't simply leave it like this,' Carnarvon said in a broken voice.

Their discovery had been the result of years of unrewarding work. Lord Carnarvon's fortune had drained away over the years, fading into the sands of the Valley as Carter had searched one site after another, never relinquishing hope, but following false trails, doomed year after year to disappointment. Carnarvon's father-in-law, Lord Rothschild, had helped with numerous donations but that source had finally dried up. Evelyn's mother, Lady Almina, had no interest in excavations: she was leading her own life with the man of her choice in Paris. Expense, and time, and humiliation . . . and now, incredible success. But the attitude of Pierre Lacau, head of the Antiquities Service, had been unbending. He would want the credit for his department and the treasures for his museums. As for the concession granted to Carnarvon, which stipulated he would be entitled to a share of treasures found in any tomb, what was that worth in reality? The Egyptian government had already demonstrated its venality, its corruption, its failure to honour commitments.

'It will be difficult, once the officials are here supervising,' Carnarvon went on in a tone edged with strain. 'If we are to obtain our rewards, we must do it now. Later, if the government honours the promises made in the concession, well, we can come back and replace in the tomb any items we have removed. Otherwise . . . is all our work to be for nothing but mere fame?'

The decision had been made.

An hour later, after Lady Evelyn and her father had gone back up to the coolness of the moonlit sands of the Valley, Callender helped Carter cover up the evidence of what they had done, and made good the breach in the wall. They filled it with loose debris, plastered over it with carefully prepared mortar. They used a replica wooden seal impression, stamped in the wet surface.

They stared in uncertainty at their crude handiwork.

'When the official visitors all come down,' Callender finally observed doubtfully, 'they'll see the work we've done. The replastering . . . it stands out like a sore thumb.'

Carter nodded. 'We can cover it with that reed basket over there. Those jars, and those loose reeds . . .'

Together they had placed the reed basket in front of the replastered hole. When the work was completed the two men had regarded each other gravely. Carter's throat was dry. 'You know, Pecky, we can never talk about this to the outside world . . . no one would understand. We will have to remain silent. For our own sakes, as well as Lord Carnarvon's.'

Up above, on the moonlit sands, they had made the pact.

But over the months, things had changed . . .

* * *

Here in the office at the Embassy Carter shifted again in his seat, angrily. The clerk still affected to ignore him, leaning over his desk, pen in hand, while the ceiling fan continued with its endless litany, *thunk, thunk, thunk* . . .

The sensation of the official opening of the tomb had been reported exclusively in *The Times*, as Carnarvon had agreed. Then seven weeks after the opening, disaster had struck: Carnarvon, Carter's patron and his friend, had died. Wild speculation immediately roared through the international press: had Carnarvon been struck down by ancient mysterious forces, labelled as the Curse of Tutankhamun? There were panics in the workforce to deal with, the presence of poison in the tomb was discussed, only to be discounted, and then, soon after the new digging season began, the interference from the Egyptian government had increased. Carter groaned deep in his throat now, as he recalled the demands of the Minister of Public Works: a bulletin to the newspapers each night before nine o'clock, denial of passes to visitors to the tomb, insistence on only bona fide scientists to be involved. And then Pierre Lacau had arrived at the tomb on a day when Carter was absent and the tomb had been locked.

He ground his teeth at the memory, and the anger stirred in him again, a sour bile of resentment rising in his throat. Work had been suspended, the concession — which had been granted to Lady Almina after her husband's death

— was changed to deny the excavators a generous share of the treasures and there had been the stormy meeting when Carter had accused the Antiquities Service of placing the work in jeopardy by incompetence, petty jealousy, ridiculous demands and inconsequential restrictions. In answer they had locked him — the discoverer of the remains of Tutankhamun — out of the tomb.

Now, it was time for bluffs to be called.

He sat there stiff-backed as from the office beyond the door a bell tinkled. The clerk lifted his head, looked at the waiting visitor and an ingratiating smile touched his lips. 'You can go in now, sir.' He rose, walked to the door behind him and opened it. 'Sir Leonard Fitzroy will see you now.'

The clerk returned to his seat as the door closed behind the visitor. He sat back in his chair, musing. Howard Carter. Probably the most famous archaeologist now, in the history of excavation, in spite of his lowly birth — the son of a water-colourist, it was said. And in spite of his lack of academic qualifications, too. Never been to university; held no archaeological honours. But it was Carter alone who had found the tomb of Tutankhamun.

The clerk shook his head. He had observed the simmering anger that lay in the man. It was well known that Carter had a violent temper, held on a notably explosive short fuse. There were others rumours, also. The talk about Lord Carnarvon's daughter, for instance . . . there were murmurs at the Club that Lady Evelyn had been very thick with Carter, in spite of the discrepancy in their ages. It would never do, of course, she would no doubt make a more appropriate marriage in due course: indeed, gossip suggested a marriage with Lord Beauchamp was in the offing. The clerk shook his head. He wondered what Howard Carter would make of that. The desert . . . it could give rise to such fanciful dreams . . .

The official suddenly became aware of the sound of raised voices in Sir Leonard's office. He was unable to hear what was actually being said, the voices were muffled, but the tone was clear. The famous Egyptologist was giving free rein, it seemed, to his frustrations and fury. He was shouting angry, unintelligible words that boomed around the walls of the office. And Sir Leonard, the clerk was shocked to realise, Sir Leonard was shouting too. The two men were clearly involved in a violent disagreement. The clerk shifted uneasily at his desk, uncertain what to do. It was unlike Sir Leonard to lose his temper: he was normally a reserved man, dignified, restrained in his views. But something had now clearly disturbed him, caused him to match Carter's violence of language.

There was a crashing sound. Now thoroughly alarmed, the clerk rose from his chair, hurried to the door, threw it open.

He was astounded by what he saw. Howard Carter was standing in front of Sir Leonard's desk, half-crouching. Sir Leonard himself, a normally cool, phlegmatic man, was on his feet shaking with rage, eyes popping in his head, glaring at his visitor.

On the wall behind Carter a large, spreading black stain had appeared, and on the floor were the shattered remains of a glass inkwell.

To his consternation, the clerk realised that it would seem that the vice-consul had thrown the inkwell at Howard Carter's head.

Stupefied, the clerk looked at the two protagonists: Sir Leonard, cheeks suffused, almost beside himself with rage, Carter also angry but with an oddly triumphant sneer on his lips. But all the stunned clerk could think of in his amazement, as he saw the black, spreading ink stain on the wall, was the state of the stained wall behind Carter.

Horrified, he calculated that the whole room would now have to be redecorated . . .

CHAPTER 1

When Eric Ward emerged from Court No. 2 he hesitated, waiting for Sharon Owen to come out into the waiting area. She had done a good job: her cross-examination of the forensic pathologist had been precise and cutting, a sharp scalpel of a performance. He tucked his briefcase under his arm and wandered across the waiting area to the broad windows that overlooked the Tyne. HMS *Northumberland,* newly painted for its goodwill visit to Newcastle, was moored just above the curving arc of the Millennium Bridge, and there was a scattering of enthusiasts waiting to accept the Royal Navy's invitation to take a tour aboard to inspect its fighting facilities. The morning sun glinted on the bright waters of the river, and the sky was blue. He took a deep breath: the weekend was looming up and he thought that maybe he ought to take the bit between his teeth and make the decision that had been at the back of his mind for some time.

A weekend away with Sharon.

He was pretty sure she'd accept such an invitation, possibly with alacrity. Sharon had dropped enough hints over the two years or more that he had known her. They'd become friends, occasionally working together when he briefed her in some of the cases that had landed on his desk, they had socialised from time to time — a dinner engagement, a trip to the Theatre Royal — and there had been occasions when he had been tempted to begin a closer relationship after something she had said, or when there had been a certain look in her eyes . . .

He found her attractive, certainly; she was bright, intelligent and sharp-witted. He liked her sense of humour, and that was something he had always felt important in a relationship. His ex-wife Anne had always had a sharp sense of the ridiculous and it had played an important part in their marriage in that they had often laughed their way out of difficulties: not their divorce of course, that had been a bad business, but even so they had managed to set aside bitterness and recover a certain balance in their relationship. They would never be able to go back to what they had, but at least they were civil to each other, friendly even, now that her former lover had left the scene. And it all seemed such a long time ago, the crumbling of their marriage, his own fall from grace, the events surrounding her relationship with her lover . . .

He shook his head, almost to clear it of disturbing memories. The sun glinted on the river and traffic pounded its way across the Tyne Bridge to his right. He heard the courtroom doors open, people coming out and he turned. Sharon was emerging from the courtroom. She was not alone: their client, the young tearaway Joe Fisher, was at her elbow and she was lecturing him in no uncertain manner. Fisher was nodding his head, his eyes fixed on hers, a half-smile on his foxy features, but Eric was pretty sure the young villain would be taking seriously very little of what she was saying. He could guess she'd be warning him: he'd come close to going down.

She made one further point and turned away. Fisher grinned, scratched his cheek, caught Eric's eye and raised an eyebrow. He made no attempt to follow Sharon as she made her way towards Eric. He watched her, nevertheless, a slight grin on his features, making no secret of his admiration for the figure of the young barrister who had just helped keep him out of jail.

'So we did it,' Sharon exclaimed as she joined Eric in front of the window.

'Their case fell apart once you demonstrated that the forensic evidence was tainted.'

'It was your brief, Eric.'

'Yes, but you skilleted the pathologist beautifully. Not that our young friend seemed to appreciate it over much.'

'Joe Fisher.' Sharon shook her head. 'I just had a word with him as we came out of court. Gave him my headmistress impression. I told him he'd got away with this one by the skin of his teeth—'

'More accurately, by the hairs on his head,' Eric suggested.

She laughed, brushed an errant blonde lock from her eyes. 'By the hairs of someone else's head, you mean. If the forensic labs hadn't messed up on the samples . . . well, that's as may be, but I think I was talking to something close to a block of wood when I warned him he couldn't expect to get away with this kind of thing again. He just stared at me, grinning, nodding his head, but it was clear his mind was on other things. But he did thank me, anyway.'

'For what that's worth.' Eric glanced sideways. Fisher was standing near the lift, talking animatedly with a red-haired man of bulky build. Slightly balding, he was perhaps ten years older than Fisher. They were laughing, clearly congratulating each other.

'You think maybe that's the other half of the team!' Sharon asked.

'If so, it's company he would be well advised to stay away from.'

'Whatever,' Sharon sighed. She looked at Eric, archly. 'We make a good team,' she suggested.

It was the perfect opportunity to put the question at the back of his mind. He put out a hand to take her arm when, just at that moment, he caught sight of Detective Sergeant Macmillan walking towards him, head lowered on broad shoulders, a bull with a red rag in sight. Macmillan had been in charge of the case against Joe Fisher. He had suffered on the stand, along with the forensic pathologist. With Macmillan was another policeman Eric recognised: Detective Chief Inspector Charlie Spate. Eric frowned as Macmillan came marching across towards him, Spate idling behind with a contemptuous twist to his mouth.

Eric had known Macmillan in the old days, before he had made it out of uniform to take up the practice on the Quayside. Macmillan had always been a stolid cop, reliable, nothing flashy, but lacking the intelligence to get anywhere further in the Force, finding his level at sergeant some years ago. He was a broad, thickset man, almost bald, his heavy brows emphasising his belligerent manner. He was glowering his displeasure now as he came up to Eric. He glanced at Sharon Owen, dismissively, then turned back to Eric. 'Bloody smart trick, you'll be thinking, no doubt.'

Eric shrugged. 'Sam, you didn't follow the correct procedures.'

'And you took advantage to let another villain back out on the street.'

'I was acting in the best interests of our client.'

'Client! I tell you, Ward, there was a time when I thought you were a good officer. When we were on the beat together I knew you could be relied on. But when you got out and walked to the other side . . .' His glance slipped back to Sharon Owen again, and he curled a contemptuous lip. 'You've crossed over Ward, and things like this aren't easily forgotten. Particularly when you pulled that trick this morning—'

'The fact is, you didn't do your homework, Sam,' Eric suggested. 'You got sloppy, didn't get things right. Those forensic reports were useless because they'd not been kept separate—'

Charlie Spate sidled forward until he stood at Macmillan's elbow, slightly taller than the detective sergeant, but equally sneering in his tone. 'Right or wrong, mistake or not, the fact is you got that young tearaway off a prison sentence he well deserved. I don't think your barrister friend here should be too pleased about it, although I suppose it's one way of ensuring you get the prospect of more fees in due course, putting a tearaway like that back on the streets.' He glanced over his shoulder at the two men entering the lift, giggling together. 'I seen plenty of their kind during my years in the Met. They'll be back to their villainy, no doubt at all. A celebration tonight probably, and then they'll be at it again. But what do you care? It's not the first time you've got in the way of what's right.'

Eric glared at Charlie Spate. They had a history. There was no love lost between the two men, and their paths had crossed often enough. No doubt they would cross again. He made no attempt to answer, began to turn away, his hand on Sharon's arm.

'You know that character that just left with Joe Fisher?' Spate asked. 'You acting for that low-life as well?'

Eric resisted the urge to reply in contempt, and remained silent, glaring at Spate, holding his glance, refusing to be intimidated or taunted into a response.

'We were acting for Mr Fisher alone,' Sharon Owen offered coldly. 'And we took what slight evidence your detective sergeant offered and showed it for what it was worth. Nothing. Now, if you'll excuse me . . .'

She nodded to Eric, tapped his hand which was still on her arm, and turned away. Eric watched her go. Thoughts of a pleasant weekend away in the Northumberland hills had vanished from his mind.

'So you don't even know that second thug,' Charlie Spate asked.

'I know him,' DS Macmillan muttered sourly. 'He's called Jag Thomas. A bad lot. Him and Fisher . . . I been watching them for some time. Thomas is the leader, thinks he knows it all. But we'll get him, and young Fisher, yet.' He grunted sourly. 'But it just shows how far down the road a good cop can go when he crosses over. You proud of yourself, Ward? I wonder what you'll think about it all when those two

16

get into something more serious, using the freedom you gave them when we could have put at least one of them behind bars!'

There was no reason why Eric should accept such comments, but equally he had no desire to get caught up in such a pointless argument. He turned on his heel, walked away from their taunts. When he emerged into the sunshine of Wesley Square, and stood beside the riverside, watching the crowd admiring the grey-painted Royal Navy boat, he still regretted not having had the chance to ask Sharon away for the weekend. But overlying that thought was the sense of irritation that he felt, a feeling that what Macmillan had said to him had some basis in fact, some rationalisation that struck a chord in Eric's own mind.

It was a dirty business, he admitted, handling cases for the dregs of the riverside. His ex-wife Anne had tried to get him to break away from this kind of clientele years ago. For a while she had succeeded. In the end it was his own stubbornness that had prevented him, but maybe she had been right. There were other fields he could be working in than criminal practice: areas other than assisting young villains to escape their just deserts. Because Eric had no doubt in his own mind. Joe Fisher had been guilty as hell. He and Sharon had got him off on a technicality.

They had only been doing their job, of course. But somehow, that was little consolation when men like Macmillan and Spate faced him with their jeering anger.

He made his way back to his office on the Quayside. He climbed the stairs, walked into the first of the rooms he rented and his secretary, Susie Cartwright, looked at him rather oddly when he entered. He felt somewhat depressed. He nodded to her, and pushed open the door to his own office. Susie was of the same mind as the others, of course. Along with his ex-wife, he thought gloomily, she thought he should be seeking a better class of business.

He settled behind his desk and with a sigh reached for the top file on the pile that Susie had left for his attention. He had barely opened it when there was a light tap on the door. He looked up: Susie stood there. She was frowning slightly. 'There was a phone call when you were at court. Mrs . . .' She hesitated. 'It was Anne.'

Susie had worked for him a long time now. She was steady, reliable, badgering on occasions like any good secretary should be, and over the years she had got to know Anne well. Susie had not approved of the marriage breakdown, and he guessed she laid most of the blame at his door. Women always stuck together, after all, he thought sourly. But ever since the divorce, she had never been quite certain how she should address Eric's ex-wife.

'Did she say what she wanted?' Eric asked.

Susie hesitated. 'She's in town for a meeting. She was checking to see if you would be in the office this afternoon. She'd like to call in to see you. I told her you were free.'

'Maybe she's going to bring me some better class of business,' Eric muttered, half to himself.

Susie glared at him. 'You could do with it, Mr Ward. But she didn't tell me why she wanted to call.'

'I'll be here anyway. No other appointments?' Susie shook her head.

'Right, so when she arrives you can show her straight in.' Eric turned back to the file he had opened. When he looked up Susie Cartwright was still standing in the doorway, somewhat uncertainly, one hand caressing her neck. Maybe she was worrying about him, like always.

'Susie? Something else?'

She hesitated. 'How did you get on this morning?'

Eric was surprised. Susie knew almost everything that was going on in the office, of course — she organised his professional life. But she rarely asked him about the cases he had been involved in, other than to check what fees were due to him, and then harass him gently about the kind of work he took on board. 'Well,' he said slowly, leaning back in his chair and linked his hands behind his head, 'I'm proud to say that it worked out pretty well, if you accept that justice was not served. Sharon Owen and I managed to wriggle around the facts, demonstrate that there was a *possibility* that the evidence was tainted, and so got a young villain off on a technicality. Something we did because it was our job, but something we shouldn't really be proud of. Not least in the view of Charlie Spate: our revered DCI had his say when the case was over.'

Susie drew a deep breath. 'I don't like DCI Spate,' she asserted.

There was something odd about her manner. She seemed edgy, nervous, and she still stood there in the doorway.

Eric shrugged. 'Well, he's not my favourite copper either. But there you go. On this occasion I have to admit he sort of had a point, however.'

Susie's glance shifted downwards, to her feet. 'So what happened to your client . . . Mr Fisher?'

Eric grunted. 'Well, let's put it like this. Young Joe Fisher was up for burglary and handling stolen goods. He wasn't alone in the break-in, but he didn't cough up any information about who was with him. Anyway, the prosecution thought they had him cold, because they were able to pick up DNA evidence from some sweat and hairs that the careless young lad had left behind him at the scene of the crime. But there was a problem with that evidence. The prosecution didn't follow the correct procedures. They bagged the evidence and sent it to the forensic people but unfortunately the stuff was hanging around, there was the chance it could have become contaminated, and Sharon was able to put the needle into the forensic witness, forcing him to admit that there was the possibility of contamination. That was all we needed. A *possibility* of tainted evidence. On such the scales of justice are balanced. The judge threw the case out. So young Joe Fisher walked free. DS Macmillan has egg on his face, Charlie Spate is confirmed in his prejudices, and I have once again achieved a victory for the lower criminal classes of this great metropolis in which we live.'

He paused, staring at Susie in puzzlement. She stood there for a few moments longer, silent. Then she touched her cheek nervously, and nodded. 'So you got him off. I just wondered, that's all.' She sighed, gathering herself for the old charge. 'But you know, Mr Ward, this isn't the kind of stuff that you should be dealing with.'

'It's the kind of *stuff* that walks into my office,' he replied. He waited. Susie hesitated, seemed to be about to say something more, and then nodded, turned, closed the door quietly behind her.

Eric was vaguely puzzled. Susie rarely showed much interest in the cases he dealt with, but he shrugged, dismissed the matter from his mind and returned to his files.

Susie came back into his office an hour later to bring him a cup of coffee but she said nothing when he thanked her. She seemed oddly preoccupied, somewhat subdued. An hour later, there was another tap on the door and his ex-wife entered the room.

Anne looked good. She was dressed in a dark business trouser suit and white blouse, and she had the air of a woman who had recently been to the hairdresser. The lines that he had observed in the months after her split with her lover, cicatrices of disappointment around her mouth, seemed to have smoothed away. She walked forward, leant over his desk as he rose and kissed him, somewhat perfunctorily, on the cheek.

'You keeping busy?'

'Can't complain, Anne.'

'Usual low-life?'

'Don't start . . . We're not going to have the old arguments, I hope.'

She laughed. 'Certainly not. It's not really my business any more, is it? How you see your future, well, that's up to you.'

Anne, and Susie, and Charlie Spate . . . and maybe Eric Ward himself, he considered sourly. 'Cup of coffee?' he asked.

She shook her head. 'No, thanks. I'm on my way back to Sedleigh Hall. Just called in because I have a favour to ask.'

'Ask away.'

She hesitated, standing in front of him, frowning slightly. 'It's quite simple, really. I wondered whether you'd be able to accompany me to an exhibition at Delamere Hall this weekend.'

'You going in for art?' he asked, surprised.

She laughed. 'No, it's nothing like that. The fact is, I've been invited to the exhibition by Colonel Delamere, who was a friend of my father's, but it's really an opportunity to make contact with some people in Durham. It could be useful in business terms. It's a weekend thing, and activities like this, well, they can turn out a bit awkward if you're by yourself, and anyway, Susie tells me you're working much too hard, so I thought a weekend away would do you good and maybe help me set something up with Peter Felshaw.'

'Who is?'

'He's a shipping agent. Offices in Sunderland and Durham. An introduction was offered, it's an opportunity to make contact . . . but it will involve dinner and I thought it might be . . .' Her voice died away. She watched him carefully. 'You don't look over enthused.'

He thrust aside thoughts of Sharon Owen. He sighed. 'I don't know Delamere, and even less about art—'

'I've told you about him,' she intervened quickly. 'And I'm not suggesting you *buy* anything, for God's sake.'

He looked at her carefully. 'A weekend at a country house. I don't know whether I want to get involved with the county set again, the way things were in the old days—'

'There are no strings, Eric,' she interrupted, flushing slightly, but he thought he detected a lack of conviction in her voice. 'Delamere knows we're divorced; he's aware you'd just be coming along as my companion, an old friend. For you, it's just a relaxed weekend away, nothing more. For me, a chance to do business.'

He felt awkward. He hadn't meant to imply that this was a subtle attempt to bring himself and Anne back together again. They both really knew that was something that was simply not going to happen. He hesitated.

'Of course,' she said coolly, 'if you feel it's a problem you could always bring your friend Sharon Owen along as company.'

She'd touched a raw nerve. 'That's all she is, Anne,' he snapped. 'A friend.'

'And all I'm seeking is a dinner companion I can trust, and one who can offer me sound advice. Although I admit that in the past I've not taken that advice . . . but then, you've already rejected mine, too.'

Eric felt they were running around in verbal circles.

He was unclear what she wanted from him: was he to be at Delamere Hall as a dinner companion or a business adviser? He voiced his uncertainty.

'A bit of both,' she replied crisply. 'I want you to accompany me, and also run your rule over Peter Felshaw. Damn it, Eric, why are you being so feeble? It's only a weekend away, in countryside I know you love. What's the problem? I've already checked with Susie and she tells me you've nothing important in your diary—'

'She checks my professional, not my social life.'

'So you have some kind of heavy date next weekend?' Anne snapped, anger staining her tone.

Eric shook his head. 'No, nothing like that. It's just that, well, it's a surprise, you asking me to join you. I mean, the way things have been the last few years—'

'We've never stopped being friends,' she commented quietly. 'And I've never lost faith in your judgment.'

He could have entered into an argument about that comment, but felt it would be unwise. He nodded in capitulation. 'All right. I'll come along to Delamere, as your right-hand man.'

'You might even enjoy it,' she declared, smiling. 'It's an exhibition of modern paintings that Jock Delamere has agreed to present in his home.'

Eric groaned.

'Don't be so dismissive,' Anne objected, shaking her head. 'It's just the colonel helping out a struggling young artist friend. Who knows, you might even see something you like.'

Eric doubted it. He doubted it very much.

* * *

Colonel Delamere was in his mid-sixties. He was a tall, spare man with hooded, thoughtful eyes, hollow cheeks and a grey, sparse moustache. He was clearly not in robust health; he stooped slightly and walked with a cane but he was carefully dressed in a grey suit, blue shirt and regimental tie, sharply creased slacks and highly polished shoes. There was an air of faded Edwardian elegance about him, the aura of the old soldier clinging to outmoded regimental values in a world he steadfastly refused to recognise as changing. Eric wondered whether he still had a batman.

He and Anne had made their way separately to Delamere Hall. When he arrived, swinging into the long curving drive that led up to the house, Eric had been impressed by the manor hall itself: Tudor in its early construction but with a wing added in the eighteenth century. It had a solid appearance that appealed to him, memories of a distant past, living with Anne at Sedleigh Hall, echoes of past grandeur. He had enjoyed living there, even though it had been with the occasional pang of guilt, for such ease of living had never sat well with his conscience. As for Delamere Hall it was clear that the colonel had endeavoured to maintain the house in good order. He was a widower, Eric gathered from Anne when he had questioned her further about the weekend invitation, living alone apart from a small retinue: a personal servant, a cook and some part-time gardeners.

Anne was already with the owner of Delamere Hall when Eric was shown into the library by a fully rigged but-ler. Anne came forward and kissed him lightly on the cheek before making the necessary introductions. Jock Delamere was polite, friendly, and his handshake was positive. He clearly knew Anne's background, and of her divorce from Eric but to him it was a matter of indifference.

'I've heard about you, Mr Ward. Anne has had many good things to say about you, and I tend to believe what she says since I've known her since she was a child. Her father was well known to me, of course. We used to hunt together, in the old days, before everything got buggered about by these Socialists. And I'm pleased that you've been able to come along to the small exhibition we have here. I've arranged for rooms to be made ready for yourself and Anne, and I hope you'll enjoy the small dinner party I've arranged . . . just for a select group of guests. Meanwhile, this afternoon there's the exhibition to look at.' He paused, smiled distantly. 'I am forced to admit that modern art of this kind is not exactly my cup of tea, but if it helps the career of a young man of whom I have heard good things and . . . well, it is necessary to assist struggling artists, is it not? One must do what one can, isn't that so, put something back into the local scene?'

It was the statement of a philanthropist, and Eric warmed to the old man, not least when he later found himself in the large room on the ground floor at the back of the house which had been set aside for the artistic works on display. The exhibits left him cold; he was unable to comprehend what most of them were meant to convey and the captions attached did little to assist him in his understanding. He was inclined to agree with Colonel Delamere's view. The work of the young man Delamere was supporting, one Daniel Meyer, simply left Eric baffled.

He listened to some of the discourse among art lovers in the room . . .

'What he imagines here in this stunning piece is the conflict between war and dreams . . . I love the manner in which Daniel has manipulated . . . with such finesse, power and perfection . . . these paintings of the nude figure to emphasise the eternal myths of humanity . . . and this one of an Icarus figure in flight with the diaphanous wings of butterflies . . . while here he portrays almost brutally a world without compass, seeking a wall lost in the mists of time . . . magnificent!'

Eric knew what Anne would say if he voiced his thoughts: he was a Philistine. So be it. The display simply wasn't Eric's cup of tea but he did his duty, spent an hour or so idling around the room, half-listening to further comments from some of the other visitors. They varied from whispered remarks of a derogatory nature to excessive yelps of delight. Colonel Delamere himself appeared from time to time, wandering in, greeting various people, making introductions that might prove useful to his young protégé, and generally supervising the situation. The young artist Daniel Meyer, when introduced to Eric, had a Gateshead accent and seemed nervous, grateful, but somewhat puzzled by the reaction of certain of his more vociferous admirers. When Eric had a brief conversation with him he discovered that the painter would not himself be attending the private dinner arranged for that evening. Colonel Delamere clearly had a line he drew in the sand: philanthropy had its limits.

'So what exactly is going on?' Eric asked Anne when he managed to corner her at one point in the late afternoon.

'I told you.' She frowned at him. 'Look, in the same way that the colonel is hoping to give this young man some assistance in his career, so he's helping me to make a business connection.' She glanced about her at one chattering group wandering about, glasses of refreshment in hand, inspecting the sculptures, several clearly puzzled by what they were supposed to represent. 'I haven't had the chance to introduce you to Peter Felshaw yet — there he is, over there. Thing is, I don't want to fuss around him too much. I want to have the chance to talk to him, but that'll be after dinner tonight. When he's mellowed a bit. Or maybe tomorrow morning, before we all leave.' She smiled. 'That's Jock Delamere's idea.'

Eric inspected the man she had pointed out. He was tall, lean in build, but with good shoulders: Eric guessed he'd be the kind of businessman who would work out regularly, as a matter of course. He was good-looking in a sharp sort of way, blue-eyed, the unruly fair hair flopping over his forehead making him look rather younger than his forty years or so. He was accompanied by a young woman: dark-skinned, dark-eyed, slight in build but endowed with a good figure and a lithe, easy stance. She was dressed in a pale beige jacket and short skirt. She had good legs too, Eric observed. He caught Anne's inquisitive, arch glance, and smiled. 'So is that Felshaw's wife?'

Anne looked across to the young woman reflectively and shook her head. 'No. She's a journalist, I understand, doing some work for Felshaw's firm. As I've brought you along, so Felshaw's brought her. The colonel likes a balanced dinner party. And a small one. In fact, this evening it will be just us two, Felshaw and that young journalist — I believe she's called Sarah — and an old friend of Colonel Delamere.'

'A woman?' Eric queried.

Anne shook her head. 'No, a writer of old acquaintance, I gather. Neil Scanlon. I met him briefly. He seems pleasant enough, if a little opinionated, a bit cocky, a bouncy sort of man. Anyway, you'll meet him tonight. He's excused himself from the exhibition.'

'As I'm going to do right now, if it doesn't appear too rude.'

'You've done your duty, Eric. I'm sure you won't be missed. Anyway, it's more or less all over now . . .'

Eric escaped into the gardens at the back of the house.

The late afternoon sun bathed the lawns in a golden light, long shadows creeping across the sward. He followed a meandering stream that led towards a copse of trees at the far end of the garden; at the edge of the wood he leant against the fence and looked out toward distant moorland. It had been a good idea, he supposed, to allow himself to be persuaded to get away for the weekend, but he still felt there was something more to Anne's invitation than she had admitted. She insisted it was merely to have a dinner companion to adhere to Delamere's idea of 'balance', but he was not entirely convinced.

No doubt he'd find out in due course.

For the moment, there was the opportunity to leave behind him the grubbiness of the clients he dealt with, and return to the kind of life and society he had enjoyed, albeit reluctantly, with Anne. If she had her way, he knew, he would enjoy it again. She had never come to terms with his decision to concentrate on his Quayside practice, rather than take advantage of the connections she could throw his way. But it was an old story, and an old argument . . .

He could hear the sound of voices from the front of the house, cars starting up, the breaking-up of the groups that had come to the exhibition. He hoped that the young artist had managed to make some sales among the county set who had come along. He walked away from the sounds and crossed the stream, made his way through the copse and leant against a tree, savouring the fresh breeze that whispered down from the hills. He wondered whether he and Sharon Owen had done Joe Fisher any favours in helping him avoid imprisonment. Somehow, he doubted it. But the police had been careless, it was their problem . . .

He thrust the thoughts away. He was supposed to be here to relax, get away from work. Or so Anne had said.

In a little while he returned to the house and made his way quietly to the room set aside for him on the second floor. Dinner was scheduled for seven in the evening. He had time to stretch out and relax for a while with a leather-bound book on Northumberland wildlife, thoughtfully placed on the bedside table, before he took a shower and dressed for dinner. Formal, Anne had specified. It was a while since Eric had donned his dinner jacket. Little use for it of recent years. The odd Law Society dinner, or an invitation from other professional societies in Newcastle. The clutter of social status.

He made his way down the broad, curved staircase a little before seven. He was directed to the library where he found Colonel Delamere already ensconced, at ease in a broad leather chair, gin and tonic in hand. Standing at his elbow, leaning on the wing of the chair, was a small, balding man in his sixties. He had ruddy features, heavy jowls, and he was tubby in build, a bantam cock, full of self-confidence. He would strut when he walked, Eric guessed. He was standing beside Delamere, rocking on his heels; he turned as Eric entered, came forward, extended his hand. 'I'm Neil Scanlon. You'll be Eric Ward. Heard about you. How's business on the Quayside?'

Eric smiled. 'Let's say it's plodding along.'

Scanlon shook his head vigorously. 'Doubt that. Lawyers always do well.'

'With the right client base,' Delamere offered.

Eric glanced at his host, suspiciously. He wondered if Anne had been saying something. But Delamere was already turning away, calling to the manservant who was dealing with the drinks. Eric had barely received his brandy and soda before Peter Felshaw entered the room and was introduced. They had little opportunity for conversation before Anne and Felshaw's companion also arrived.

'Ha! The full complement,' Colonel Delamere beamed. 'Everyone on time. Even the ladies. This is the way I like things: a sense of what is proper, an old bachelor friend of long standing—' he gestured towards Scanlon '—to keep this aged widower in check and a small group of distinguished friends and acquaintances to spend a pleasant evening together. Now, the only introduction still necessary is to you, young lady.' He turned to Peter Felshaw's companion. 'You haven't yet met Mr Ward.'

Peter Felshaw's companion came forward, extended her hand and smiled. 'I'm Sarah Castle. And you're a lawyer I believe.'

'While you are a journalist,' Eric countered.

'Of sorts.'

'I normally try to avoid saying much to journalists.'

She laughed. She had good teeth, and her voice was light and pleasant. 'Well, you'll have to make an exception, for once. In such a small group over dinner you'll have to be polite to me.'

'I wouldn't regard it as difficult,' Eric said. Her eyes held his for a few moments, appraisingly. Then she turned aside, to accept a drink from the waiter. Neil Scanlon took the floor as though he expected it as a matter of course.

'So, Mr Felshaw, you're in the shipping business, I understand.'

Felshaw nodded. 'I'm a director of a shipping agency, on the south bank of the Tyne.'

'Delamere was telling me. Plenty of business these days, it seems.' Scanlon's voice had a booming quality, almost aggressive as though he was constantly demanding his word be taken as gospel. 'It's surprising how much freighting is done on the Tyne. In the old days of coal and shipbuilding the river was crammed, but after those industries collapsed there was talk of decline. Yet other businesses have come in, the riverside is being developed, freighters arrive from all over the world . . . but I gather you've been having some problems recently.'

Peter Felshaw sipped his drink carefully. 'How do you mean?'

'I understand you've been getting a certain amount of trouble at Jarrow.'

'We've had a couple of visits from the police, that's for certain,' Felshaw agreed, nodding.

'What's been the difficulty?' Neil Scanlon asked.

Felshaw shrugged dismissively. 'Various events, some irritating, some rather more serious. Suspicious packages delivered to the agency in Jiffy bags. A failed firebomb. Amateur stuff, really. Nothing important. We have a pretty good security service, and they didn't breach it.'

'Are you talking about explosive devices?' Eric asked.

'Not really dangerous, scary rather. As I say, amateur stuff. But then there was the arson attempt . . . that could have been serious.' Felshaw shook his head. 'As it happened, there was no one in the office at the time, the sprinkler system worked effectively, and it was just a matter of losing a few files.'

'Do you have any idea who might be behind the attacks?' Eric asked curiously.

Felshaw scratched his chin. 'The police have a view. They think it's down to a group of thugs they know about. On the other hand . . .'

There was a dismissiveness in Felshaw's tone that should have ended the conversation but Scanlon clung to his target with a surprising persistence. 'Do you think it'll have anything to do with the fact that your firm is Jewish-owned?' he challenged.

There was a short pause. Felshaw stared at his drink. Sarah Castle glanced across at Eric and smiled slightly, raised an eyebrow. Eric caught a glimpse of the shadow of annoyance that touched Colonel Delamere's eyes, and he wondered about the relationship between the two old men. Delamere had described Scanlon as an old friend, yet they seemed so unlike each other: Delamere urbane, polite, friendly; Scanlon strutting, pompous, self-regarding, never reluctant to tread heavily on delicate matters.

Felshaw considered the question for a few moments longer before he answered. He raised one shoulder in a careless shrug. 'I'm afraid we haven't really spent much time considering the reasons behind the . . . unpleasantness. We recently had to get rid of a few employees who had been causing us problems, and the police are looking into that, and other possibilities . . .'

Sarah Castle edged forward to turn the question around on Scanlon. 'Why do you think it might be a matter of ownership of the firm?'

Scanlon grinned, pleased to have caught the attention of the group. 'It's simply my enquiring mind. I often see reasons others don't: conspiracies abound in this world and I enjoy rooting them out. It simply occurred to me that maybe these incidents occurred because there's been a raised interest in the Jewishness of Mr Felshaw's firm in view of the current state of the peace process in the Middle East.'

'We're in the east of England,' Colonel Delamere scoffed warningly, 'not the Middle East.' He set his glass down on the table beside him. 'Don't you think—'

'I think it's a *possibility,*' Scanlon interrupted, with a mocking smile at his host. 'Jock, you're way out of date; you don't keep up with world politics, you've vegetated since you devoted your attention to Delamere Hall twenty years ago. I bet you're hardly aware even that there's a peace process in hand. In spite of us both having spent years out in Cairo. The main protagonists now have at last started to do something they should have done years ago.'

'You're talking about the London Conference,' Sarah Castle suggested.

Colonel Delamere seemed on the point of interrupting, to suggest that there might be more suitable, non-contentious conversations to have in such company, but then subsided as Neil Scanlon spread his legs wide, stood squarely in front of the young journalist and waved his glass airily. 'The breakthrough's been a long time coming in the Middle East, but the odds have improved considerably of recent times. Once Israel said they'd treat seriously plans that would envisage Arab recognition of their country in exchange for Israel's withdrawal from territory occupied in the 1967 war—'

'You really think that would be workable?' Delamere growled, almost to show that Scanlon's criticism had been unfounded.

'I say it's a possibility, unless some new flashpoint comes up to get the sides at each other's throats again,' Scanlon insisted. 'And there are always young thugs out there trying to cause trouble, stir up feelings, bring attention to what they see as their causes by sending things like firebombs through the post in the hope that they could bring about some noise and alarm. That's why I thought maybe the trouble Mr Felshaw's been having—'

'I don't think it's anything to do with the London Conference, Mr Scanlon.' Felshaw shook his head soberly. 'Too localised and small scale. Who pays attention to petty villains along the Tyne — other than the local police, of course.'

'But what do you think is new about the talks?' Sarah Castle asked quietly of Scanlon.

Scanlon puffed out his chest and placed one hand on his expansive belly, drumming his fingers on the faded red cummerbund he affected. 'Several facts — notably America's new anxiety for Arab support in its Middle East adventures . . . about which we all have views, no doubt! The USA is prepared for almost the first time, in my view, to put serious pressure on its old ally.'

'Israel is still not budging on its refusal to grant the right to all Palestinians to return home,' Felshaw commented. 'That's still a sticking point.'

'That's right, but the negotiations could bring about a change . . .'

'The status of Jerusalem will still be a major barrier to any final agreement,' Sarah Castle suggested.

Scanlon nodded vigorously. 'But at least the two sides are talking, with the USA, Britain and France shoving them together. There's no doubt been a thaw in relationships: it's now time for real agreements to be reached. The Palestinian government has struck a deal, it seems, internally. Fatah and Hamas representatives are sitting at the same table and Israel seems less inflexible than formerly over dealings with these groups — who've been fighting with each other as much as anyone else of recent years. But ever since the operating hours of the Karni cargo crossing at Gaza were extended — a lifeline for the impoverished area — there's been a relaxation of tension.'

'There's many a slip,' Sarah Castle commented. 'Just one little thing could send both sides reaching for their guns again . . .'

'But hardly a failed firebomb directed at Mr Felshaw's offices,' Eric suggested.

'And County Durham is a long distance away from London, and even further from the Middle East,' Colonel Delamere commented. 'Another round of drinks? Ladies? Gentlemen? In ten minutes we can proceed through to the dining room.'

He seemed relieved to get away from the subject Neil Scanlon had raised.

* * *

There was something old-worldly about Colonel Delamere as he presided over dinner. He sat at the head of the table, beaming and relaxed, as the two white-jacketed waiters, clearly hired for the occasion, flitted discreetly in and out of the room with the dishes and the wine. He had placed Anne on his right and Sarah Castle on his left but he made no attempt to monopolise them in conversation. Rather he leant back in his chair much of the time, observing his guests, obviously taking pleasure in the flow of conversation about him, happy that he should have been able to take the opportunity to bring together a group of such friends and acquaintances. Knowing only Anne previously among the group, Eric felt slightly at odds at first but settled well enough into a desultory conversation with Peter Felshaw on his left and Sarah Castle on his right. He still felt slightly uneasy, still not certain what he was doing there at all. Anne had asked him to give her a view about Felshaw. As far as Eric was able to make out he seemed a pleasant enough fellow, and the earlier conversation before dinner had suggested to Eric that Felshaw was a man who would keep his own counsel on business matters, even if he were provoked. Neil Scanlon had certainly attempted to do just that, Eric felt, but Felshaw had been non-committal.

As for Anne, she said very little to him. She was in sparkling form, talking mostly with Neil Scanlon and her host and paying little attention to Peter Felshaw, even though Eric knew that it was Felshaw who had provided her with the excuse for coming to this dinner party and dragging him along. But he was aware that Felshaw watched her in his turn, and Eric knew her well enough to guess she was out to make a good impression. And she seemed to be doing just that. She was still a beautiful woman, not in a conventional way perhaps, but there was a lightness about her tonight that sent his thoughts spinning back over the years to when they had first met, and when they had fallen in love.

But Sarah Castle was a beautiful woman too, and Colonel Delamere was clearly well satisfied by his choice of companions. Sarah's dark looks were set off by the white dress she wore, and the colonel had provided both women with a red corsage. He clearly clung to traditions of the old school — dinner-jacketed men, women in formal evening dress attire. The county set that Eric had become disenchanted with years ago had always insisted upon such formalities, but somehow here, in Delamere Hall, they seemed right, and acceptable.

'I rarely have the opportunity to attend a pleasant dinner such as this back home,' Sarah Castle murmured, leaning slightly towards Eric so that her shoulder touched his lightly.

'Just where is your home?' Eric asked.

'Oh, here and there really. I was raised in the States—'

'I wouldn't have picked that up from your accent.'

'Cosmopolitan. My parents travelled a lot. I even had a short period in a ladies' finishing school in England.' She chuckled; it had a deep, pleasant ring to it. 'I think the headmistress was pleased when I left. Too headstrong for her nerves.'

'So you were a wild young thing?' Eric asked, smiling.

'Nothing serious. A little too unconventional, shall we say, for her peace of mind.'

'And after that?'

She shrugged, sipped her wine. 'A short while in Germany; two years in Paris, and eventually a year in Stockholm.'

'At work?'

She shook her head. 'No. My father was a civil servant, a diplomat of sorts. That took us to the States, to Paris, to Hamburg.'

'And Stockholm?'

'Ah . . .' She glanced at him, mischief twinkling in her eyes. 'That was later. There was a man.'

There seemed little Eric could say by reply.

Neil Scanlon had decided to return to the topic that had engaged him before dinner. He addressed his remarks to Felshaw, a dog worrying at his bone. 'This question of anti-Semitism in the matter of the attacks upon your firm—'

'I wasn't aware that we had decided it was a matter of anti-Semitism,' Felshaw demurred, with a smile that seemed a little forced. 'But who can say at this stage? As I said earlier, I'm inclined to let the police get on with it. They know what they're doing.'

'More than our politicians seem to,' Scanlon commented. 'I'm afraid I've little confidence in the representatives they've identified for the London Conference. Coming back to that, what do your board of directors feel about that initiative, Felshaw?'

The shipping agent raised his eyebrows in mock dismay. 'You can hardly spring a question like that on me with any hope of an answer, sir. Does any employer ever know what's in the minds of his board of directors?'

'But you must have your own view.'

Felshaw hesitated, a slight frown crossing his brow. 'Well, for what it's worth, I think the conference is maybe a first step to real peace. God knows we've waited long enough for something positive to come out of that part of the world. The fact that both Hamas and Fatah have agreed, albeit reluctantly, to sit around a table with representatives of the Israeli and American governments, as well as their own, to discuss peace in the Middle East, is a huge step in itself, given recent events.'

'Don't forget our own part in it,' Scanlon advised. Felshaw inclined his head in agreement. 'Of course.'

'It was the British who prepared the protocols, and made the initial approaches. And of course, they've long had an interest in the Arab-Israeli conflict.'

'Which some would say they were largely responsible for,' Scanlon suggested. 'After all, let's face it, the British were behind most of the problems back in the twenties. End of Empire and all that. The promise to the Arabs, and then the Balfour Declaration.'

Colonel Delamere snorted. He clearly had his own views about the politicians of another era. 'The Balfour Declaration! It's always been a mystery to me how Balfour was persuaded to enter into that statement of intent. Of course he had Churchill and Lloyd George at his elbow. A powerful triumvirate.'

Sarah turned her head to look at her host. Her eyes seemed very green, Eric thought. 'I've always understood the British government made that declaration, supporting a Jewish homeland, because they wanted to secure the complete loyalty of Zionist Jews in Britain and America. It was a way of persuading the USA to enter into the First World War.'

'Oh, I think it was all rather more complicated than that,' Scanlon disagreed loftily. 'Indeed, my own recent researches would suggest that there was a certain conspiracy that had been established in December 1916—'

He was clearly about to launch himself upon some long-held theory that was already familiar to his host. Colonel Delamere smiled, held up a warning hand, clearing his throat. There was a certain amused cynicism in his tone. 'Ladies, gentlemen, I should warn all those present that Neil is one of that suspicious group of people who are commonly called conspiracy theorists. He and I, as old friends, have certainly discussed Arab-Israeli relations and the part played by Britain in the crises of 1916 on many occasions — and the consequences that have echoed down the decades ever since. He's prepared to talk at great length about these views at dinner parties — unless his host takes steps to prevent him.'

He smiled at Scanlon who seemed to have taken no offence. 'Neil talks endlessly about these events but he's never actually written about them. On the other hand, he's written much about many other conspiracies.'

'Such as?' Sarah Castle leant forward. Beside her, Eric was aware of the line of her throat, and the lowness of the cut of her dress.

Colonel Delamere smiled mischievously. 'You're a stranger here, Miss Castle. You wouldn't be aware perhaps that Neil Scanlon is an eminent author. Or so he tells me, regularly.'

'Not eminent. Internationally famous,' Scanlon suggested, grinning, leaning back in his chair, and clearly satisfied that he was the centre of attention.

Delamere beamed at his friend. 'Of course, it may be that some among you have already read certain of his books: Lincoln's murder and the immediate, suspicious killing of his murderer John Wilkes Booth — it was all down to the Secretary of State, it seems. According to Neil, the Kennedy assassination was a Texan right-wing coup. The death of Diana, Princess of Wales, well, of course that was all a massive cover-up by MI5.' There was a certain condescension in his tone. 'It is, after all, how Neil's made a living for a number of years.'

Sarah Castle sighed. 'Ah, you're *that* Neil Scanlon.'

'I would be disappointed if I were thought to be any other,' Scanlon replied airily. He was clearly unfazed by the mockery in Delamere's tone, or the amusement in the young woman's. 'Conspiracy theorist if you like. I prefer to be regarded as a seeker after truth . . .'

'Which necessarily always involves a mystery and a climactic, world-shattering event,' Delamere opined.

Scanlon waved his wineglass in easy assent. 'Mysteries sell books,' he advised, 'and people like to believe that all is not as it seems from official explanations.'

'You really *believe* in these theories?' Felshaw intervened.

'I'm out to sell books,' Scanlon replied easily. 'It doesn't matter if what I write is actually true — it's enough that legitimate questions are raised—'

'—and leaps of faith and suspension of judgment called for,' Sarah laughed outright.

'Don't *you* turn against me as well as everyone else,' Scanlon complained in mock protest. 'Am I all alone in this room?'

'So what are you working on at the moment?' Eric asked as the others joined in the laughter. He himself was aware of the skill and casual ease with which Colonel Delamere had moved the conversation away from Felshaw's troubles and the politics of the Middle East.

He also had the vague feeling that it had been deliberate, as though Delamere had not cared for the direction in which the earlier conversation had been heading. Perhaps he had been seeking to avoid Felshaw embarrassment. Scanlon observed Eric quietly for a few seconds then lifted a shoulder deprecatingly, clucked his tongue. 'It's early days, and some would consider the subject is a bit old hat.'

'What is the subject?' Felshaw asked. Eric glanced at him. Just as Delamere had been pleased at the change in topic, so Eric seemed to detect a hint of relief in the shipping agent's eyes.

Scanlon shifted his own glance around at his dinner companions, smiling at each in turn. 'My subject? I suppose you could say it's based on the Curse of the Pharaohs.'

'Oh, dear me,' Delamere mocked, rocking back in his chair. 'Really, Neil, surely that's been worked out, pummelled to death. The discovery of Tutankhamun's tomb and all that, the death of Lord Carnarvon, hacks jumping on the bandwagon to compete with even more sensational stories about mysterious happenings . . .' He reached for his wineglass and made a great show of taking a fortifying sip.

Scanlon observed him with a certain detachment, smiling as if recognising the waywardness of a favourite child. 'If Carnarvon had survived, I've no doubt *he* would have believed in the curse. He was an active member of the London Spiritual Alliance, did you know? He often took part in and even organised séances. It was quite the vogue at the time.'

'Perhaps because of the horrific experiences of the First World War,' Sarah murmured soberly.

'Even so,' Scanlon admitted. 'But after the tomb was opened there was certainly a series of events—'

Sarah sipped at her own wine, and in a gently mocking tone said, 'Don't tell us. At Carnarvon's death all the lights mysteriously went out in Cairo, his favourite Highland terrier howled, keeled over and died as though struck by lightning, Howard Carter's canary was eaten by a cobra, and then the romance writer Marie Corelli warned she had known all along of the dire consequences that would follow upon the opening of the tomb.' Her tone was teasing as she nodded towards her host. 'As a journalist myself, I have to agree with your comment about hacks, Colonel Delamere. There was certainly a media frenzy at that time among journalists who had been denied access to first-hand accounts of the tomb excavations and yet still had to sell papers somehow. But it all became rather silly; people took the stories at face value, they even started sending Egyptian artefacts to museums rather than keep them, for fear that the curse might be visited upon them.'

Scanlon shrugged. 'There were a number of . . . coincidences. Carnarvon's half-brother died—'

'After a visit to the dentist,' Sarah laughed. 'But such visits are a curse in themselves, aren't they?'

'There were other inexplicable occurrences,' Scanlon bridled slightly, taking up the challenge. 'The railroad magnate Jay Gould died of pneumonia after visiting the tomb of Tutankhamun as did the French Egyptologist Georges Benedite. Then there was Howard Carter's colleague Arthur Mace, and take the case of Ali Kemel Fahmy Bey—'

'Shot by his wife in the Savoy Hotel,' Sarah demurred. Scanlon was undeterred. 'Then there was Carnarvon's other half-brother . . .'

'I'm sure it was all media frenzy and nothing more,' Sarah assured him. 'A kind of Tutmania. At least, that's what one gathers from reading Thomas Hoving's book, and the recent work by James—'

Scanlon stopped her by holding up his hands in mock amazement. 'I'm impressed,' he said, nodding his head in admiration. 'You've really read the literature. I must take you on as my research assistant.'

She shrugged. 'It would bore me to death,' she asserted. 'So the money would have to be good. As to the literature . . . I'm a journalist. It's something we all go through at some time or another — reading about the big stories of the past.'

Scanlon's eyes narrowed, and he leant back confidently in his chair. He was enjoying what he saw as a contest, Eric guessed. 'Miss Castle, you can't really believe I'd be concentrating on all that stuff, rehashing old, fanciful, imagination-stretching stories.'

'So what is it you're going to be working on?' Anne asked. 'Something Mr Ward might be interested in, being a lawyer.'

'Me?' Eric asked in surprise.

Scanlon nodded. 'The name of Bethell will be familiar to you, I imagine.'

Eric agreed. 'Of course. A well-known legal family. I'm assuming you're talking of Richard Bethell, Lord Chancellor, raised to the peerage as Lord Westbury. Or his son, also called Richard.'

'Irritating, for a historian, the way these people always called their sons after themselves,' Delamere commented, happy enough with the way in which the conversation seemed to have engaged the attention of all the group seated at table.

'Family tradition,' Eric explained.

'Quite. But awkward . . . one Richard Bethell after another. Confusing.'

'So what exactly are you looking at in relation to that family?' Eric queried.

'Their involvement in the Curse of the Pharaohs,' Scanlon replied blandly.

There was a short silence. Sarah smiled and seemed about to say something, but glanced at Eric and then held her peace. Eric noted a small frown of concern had appeared on Colonel Delamere's features as he leant forward and topped up her wineglass. 'Still the curse . . .'

Scanlon was unaffected. 'There really *was* a Bethell connection, you know. Between Lord Chancellor Westbury, Carter, and the tomb of the boy-king Tutankhamun.'

Eric was interested, in spite of himself. 'Just what was the connection?'

'Mr Ward, don't encourage my old friend,' Delamere warned.

Surprisingly, it was Anne who supplied the connection. She had been listening with a slight smile on her lips but now she frowned and in a serious tone she said, 'Didn't I read somewhere that Richard Bethell, Lord Westbury's son, happened to have been private secretary to Lord Carnarvon?'

Scanlon nodded, satisfied. 'That was certainly the case. Young Dick Bethell was present at the excavations and was there when the tomb was opened in December 1922.'

'You're not going to tell us that he was struck down by the Curse of the Pharaohs,' Delamere muttered, almost grumbling.

Scanlon shook his head. 'Not exactly. Richard Bethell died some years later, in 1929, when much of the frenzy about the Pharaoh's Curse had died down, except among bored journalists looking for copy. But the circumstances of his death were, shall we say, rather unusual . . .'

'He died in Egypt?' Eric asked curiously.

Scanlon shook his head, and drained his wineglass. There was a slight flush to his pudgy cheeks now, but he was well launched. 'No. His demise occurred at the Bath Club in London.'

'At some remove from the tomb, then,' Sarah observed, glancing at Eric with a twinkle in her green eyes. 'Though according to the hacks of the day, the ancient curse could cross continents. Quite how the old Egyptians managed to plan for that has never been explained, of course.'

Unabashed, Scanlon went on, 'Certainly. But I reiterate. It's not the old hat stuff about the Curse of the Pharaohs that I'm interested in. No, it's really the circumstances surrounding the death of the Lord Chancellor's son. It is noteworthy that Richard had brought back with him many relics and mementoes from the tomb of Tutankhamun. He kept them in his house. And after his death, Lord Westbury was frequently heard to utter the words *the Curse of the Pharaohs* in connection with his son's death.'

'Mere superstition,' Delamere scoffed.

'And you just said it wasn't the curse you were interested in,' Eric reminded him.

Scanlon ignored the interruptions. In a soberly dogged tone, he said, 'And then, just three months after Richard's death, Lord Westbury himself died.'

'He was, I believe, about seventy-nine years of age,' Sarah Castle commented. But she was not looking at Scanlon; her eyes were on Colonel Delamere. There was something reflective about her glance.

'Was his age relevant?' Scanlon queried. 'The fact is, he didn't die in bed — he fell to his death from the balcony of his seventh-storey apartment in St James's Court, in west London. He crashed into a glass veranda; he almost severed his head, but it was the impact on the pavement below that killed him.'

Sarah flicked a fingernail on the rim of her half-empty wineglass. The resulting ring echoed around the room. She smiled. 'There was a suicide note, I believe.'

She appeared to have taken on the role of advocate for the defence, Eric considered. Certainly, Scanlon seemed to be addressing his comments to her personally now, as though they were involved in some private skirmish. 'There was. It read *I cannot stand any more horrors.*'

Sarah turned to Eric. 'Hardly explicit, hey, Mr Ward?'

Eric shrugged non-committally. 'Evidence of a state of mind, I suppose.'

'But not really expressive of the *reason* for his suicide,' Sarah insisted.

'If it *was* suicide,' Scanlon commented, not to be denied.

Colonel Delamere seemed vaguely uneasy. In the short silence that followed Scanlon's loaded comment he stared fixedly at his dinner guest. 'Are you seriously suggesting Lord Westbury did not kill himself in a state of depression after the death of his son?'

Scanlon held his glance, one eyebrow raised quizzically. 'I've no answer to that, not yet. I'm still pursuing my researches . . .'

'Into a death some eighty years after the event?' Eric queried.

Scanlon chuckled. 'Into the events — and situations that arose at the *time* of his death,' he corrected. 'No, it's not the ancient Curse of the Pharaohs that interests me. That, so to speak, has been done to death. The mystery I'm delving into, the conspiracy theory I'm working on . . .'

'Like always,' Colonel Delamere moaned to his old friend.

'It's whether or not Richard Bethell and his father Lord Westbury were in fact *murdered*.'

Their wineglasses were empty. There was a silence around the table for a few moments. Colonel Delamere seized his opportunity. He rose from his chair. 'On that note, I think we might all with profit leave the topic where it lies . . . looking forward to the eventual emergence of Neil's next informative book. I suggest we would all now find solace in a coffee while we mull over what strange byways a dinner party can lead us into, in matters of conversation. Ladies . . . I think I may accommodate both of you, as your host and an elderly one to boot . . .'

The women rose, each took one arm, and Colonel Delamere led the way out of the dining room. Over his shoulder he added, 'For those who are that way inclined, a brandy is available with the coffee in the drawing room.' He glanced amiably at each of the ladies beside him. 'And we won't observe the Victorian and Edwardian custom of expecting the ladies to retire from our company. They shall continue to adorn our party.'

* * *

The following morning, after a light breakfast, Eric strolled out onto the terrace. It was promising to be a bright day, though there was a slight chill in the early breeze. He paced up and down for a short while, uncertain what to do. Just before the dinner party had broken up the previous evening, Colonel Delamere had taken Eric to one side.

'Do you have anything pressing on Sunday?' he had asked.

Eric shrugged. 'Nothing in particular. My intention had been to take a run out to the coast, maybe up to Druridge Bay, before returning to Newcastle.'

Colonel Delamere had nodded soberly. 'So if I were to ask you to stay on for the morning, that would not be a problem?'

'Certainly not. Is there something you wish to discuss with me?'

Delamere had nodded thoughtfully. 'I shall be working on some papers for an hour or so after breakfast — I'm far too tired right now. After that, maybe at about eleven in the morning, perhaps we could have a little while together?'

Eric had agreed, without asking any questions about the nature of their meeting, but in the warm sunlight of the morning he began to wonder again whether he detected the hand of his ex-wife in Delamere's suggestion. He glanced at his watch: nine-thirty. He had more than an hour to spend before his scheduled meeting, so he might as well go for a walk. He was about to go down the steps from the terrace when he heard the door open behind him. He glanced over his shoulder: Sarah Castle was emerging, smiling at him.

He realised that there was a russet tone to her dark hair where the sunlight caught it. She was dressed in a light roll-neck sweater, jeans and tan boots. The jeans seemed moulded to her legs; the sweater, though not tight, nevertheless displayed her figure to advantage.

'I didn't see you at breakfast,' he said.

'Too lazy. Slept in. And I'm not too crazy about breakfast anyway.' She came forward, stood beside him, shorter by no more than a few inches. She looked about her and gave a sigh of satisfaction. 'I don't know Northumberland really,' she admitted. 'From what I've seen of it, it's a beautiful area.'

'Hills, moors, beaches and castles,' he agreed. 'We just keep quiet about it so it doesn't get overwhelmed by tourists.'

She nodded. 'So are you about to leave for your home? Which is . . . where?'

'I've got an apartment in Newcastle. No, I'm not leaving yet for a while. The colonel wants to see me.'

'Is that so?'

'And you?'

She shrugged. 'I didn't come up here under my own steam. Peter drove. So now I have to wait for him. He's meeting your wife—'

'Ex-wife.'

She laughed. 'Sorry. I forgot. Ex-wife. She seems a nice person.'

'She is.'

'But you decided you couldn't live together.'

'Something like that.' Sarah Castle, he decided was a very frank woman. 'You have any idea how long Felshaw is going to be with Anne?'

'At least another hour, I would imagine. They're talking business. Your ex-wife proposes to take an interest in the shipping agency business. She's quite an entrepreneur, I believe.'

'She has plenty of activities to keep her occupied.' He hesitated. 'If you're waiting, and I'm waiting . . .'

She glanced at him, raising an interrogative eyebrow. 'Yes?'

'I was about to go for a walk. Perhaps you'd like to join me?'

'That would be very pleasant,' she said decisively.

They followed the route Eric had taken the previous afternoon. They crossed the small stream but avoided the copse, to climb the low hill that led to the range of moorland that dominated the skyline. At the top of the hill they reached a rocky ridge and the countryside opened out about them. In the distance they could just make out the hazy outline of the coast. They sat close together on the crag, saying little, enjoying the view.

Sarah broke the silence. 'So what did you make of Colonel Delamere's friend last night?'

'Scanlon.' Eric laughed, but chose his words with care. 'I think he's an intelligent, able man, probably a good writer, in his own field, but perhaps a little too full of himself. It's a curious relationship, though, he and the colonel. They're so very different in character.'

'Yes . . . How does the colonel strike you?'

Eric glanced at her. The light breeze was ruffling her dark hair, and she thrust it back with impatience. 'He's very much a man of the old school, I think. Army background, knows right from wrong, isn't the kind of person who'd break away from his principles, honest, straightforward . . .'

'You liked him. A paragon,' she mocked. 'The kind of man you English admire as the norm. So we have the colonel . . . and we have Neil Scanlon.'

'Who would likely throw scruples overboard if he could get a narrative out of it,' Eric laughed.

'What did you think about his new research?'

'Into whether or not the Bethells, father and son, were murdered? It's more than eighty years ago, and I think he's wasting his time.' He glanced at her curiously. 'But you seemed to know as much about it as anyone.'

She nodded, her eyes fixed on the far horizon. 'I suppose so. And eighty years is a long time. But it's a strange thing . . . the past never really leaves you. It's like leaves blowing in the wind: they settle, for a while, until the next gust comes along and lifts them to skitter along the boardwalk again.'

'But are you giving credence to his suspicion that Richard Bethell and Lord Westbury were murdered? Just because there was a connection between them and Lord Carnarvon doesn't give rise to a motive for murder. Even in view of the Curse of the Pharaohs.'

She laughed and shook her head. 'Oh, I doubt that it's anything to do with the so-called curse. But it might have something to do with artefacts taken from the tomb.'

'By whom?' Eric asked, surprised.

Sarah looked at him, eyes widening in mock surprise. 'You're not going to tell me you're clinging to the idea that Englishmen are all models of good behaviour, and would never do anything underhand, to the disgrace of King and Country! You don't think Howard Carter and Lord Carnarvon were squeaky clean, do you?'

'They were devoted archaeologists, and—'

'And not above a bit of skulduggery! Come off it, Eric,' she scoffed. 'It's been known for decades that Carter, Carnarvon, his daughter and a friend of theirs called Callender, entered the tomb before the official opening. It is also widely accepted nowadays that they removed certain items from the tomb on that occasion. Some they returned, to the satisfaction of Pierre Lacau of the Antiquities Service, but others they kept for their own private collection.'

'I wasn't aware of that.'

'The American Egyptologist Thomas Hoving even made a careful list of the items: they included gold nails, faience beads, collars, paint palettes, bronze and gold arte-facts, including one of a magnificent leaping horse.'

'But how—'

'Hoving could make the list because the items later came onto the market.' She shrugged, almost wearily. 'The American market, of course. The Metropolitan Museum paid $145,000 for Carnarvon's collection. That's more than $14 million in today's money. It's known to have included items from the tomb of Tutankhamun. Specifically, there are the two faience rings — items Carter noted he had found on the floor of the tomb — which were sold by the Carnarvon estate in 1926. Other pieces ended up in the Cincinnati Museum, the Brooklyn Museum and the Cleveland Museum of Art.'

Eric was silent for a little while. He had never read much about the excavations at the tomb in the early twentieth century. And he had held an image of intrepid excavators, devoted to science. 'But where does the Bethell family fit in? What's it got to do with them?'

'Ah, well, we have the published evidence of a certain Count Louis Hamon in 1934 that Lord Carnarvon took numerous relics from the tomb and sent them to England. Moreover, the said Count Hamon stated that Lord Westbury confided to him that his son Richard, secretary to Lord

Carnarvon, brought back with him many relics and mementoes from Tutankhamun's tomb. Hamon also reckoned he had seen some of these relics on nearly every wall of Lord Westbury's home. They had been removed by Carter and Carnarvon, and found their way into the Bethell household.'

'You surprise me. I always thought . . . but taking items from the tomb, why would Carter and Carnarvon put their reputations at such risk?'

Sarah Castle lowered her head, shrugged slightly. She picked up a loose piece of rock and threw it down the crag; it bounced and rattled its way downward until it came to rest in the hillocky grass. 'It might have been simply they were caught up in the lucrative market in such artefacts; it might have been due to the bitterness and resentment they felt at the behaviour of the Antiquities Service and the Egyptian government. And there were the terms of the concessions which made it uncertain whether Carnarvon — or his widow, as it happened — would ever receive any share of the treasures from the tomb. Right or wrong, it was probably the case that they both felt they were owed remuneration for all the years of hard work they had spent in the Valley of the Kings.'

'But is this merely supposition?' Eric queried doubtfully.

'Not really. Their behaviour came to the notice of the Egyptologist Arthur Weigall quite early on. He was a journalist employed by the *Daily Mail*. It's a matter of record that he wrote bluntly to Carter in 1923, complaining of his conduct: he charged that Carter opened the tomb before notifying the government representative . . . and so had the opportunity of stealing some millions of pounds' worth of gold . . .'

'And you're saying that some of the stolen items ended up with Richard Bethell and Lord Westbury?'

'That's about the size of it. And that brings Scanlon to his investigations into the death of Bethell and his father.'

'I still don't follow—'

'Oh, you have to remember Neil Scanlon is a purveyor of conspiracy theories. If I had to make a guess, I would say he's going to suggest that there was something special that was handed to the Bethells, apart from the bronze and gold artefacts. Special . . . of great value . . . and maybe even dangerous.'

'How do you mean?'

'It would be something that Carter took from the tomb. He gave it to them to hold for him. He placed it in their safe keeping.'

'I don't understand.'

'It was something Carter did not dare keep himself. Something too valuable. By banding it to the Bethells, a legal family and a powerful one at that, he might have felt the item could have been kept more secure.'

'Against what?'

She looked at him and smiled. 'Who knows? Neil Scanlon will no doubt come up with an answer. And equally, no doubt, it will be something earth-shattering in the way of a conspiracy theory. And he'll say — if I had to make another guess — that it was the reason why Richard Bethell and his father had to die.' She watched him carefully, as though she was weighing something up in her mind and then suddenly she stood up, looked at her watch. 'Anyway, we'll all find out in due course, no doubt, when Scanlon finishes his book. I think now, Eric, we ought to get back to the hall. Peter and Anne should have finished by this time.'

They made their way back down towards the house. On the terrace, Sarah turned, put a hand out. 'Thank you for your company. I enjoyed our walk. And meeting you.'

'We must do it again some time.'

She looked at him levelly, a certain challenge in her eyes. 'Why not?'

'How can I get in touch with you?' Eric asked.

'I'll contact you,' she said, smiling. 'Now, I'd better find out what's happening about my lift back to County Durham.'

After she had gone Eric remained on the terrace a little while, thinking over what she had told him. He had severe doubts that the story Scanlon might spin of the mysterious deaths of the Bethells would have any sound basis in reality, but it might make an interesting narrative. And as Scanlon had stated, mysteries sold books.

He was interrupted by the butler, dressed now less formally than on the previous evening. 'Coffee is waiting in the library, Mr Ward. Colonel Delamere will be able to join you there in a few minutes.'

Eric thanked him, and made his way to the library.

He had paid little attention to the books held there during his earlier visit the previous evening. Now, as he sipped his coffee, he wandered along the lengths of shelves. It was an eclectic collection. Naturally enough there were many books on the theme of war; some military histories, some manuals on particular items of artillery. There was quite a collection of books on ancient history and he was amused to see several of Neil Scanlon's volumes holding pride of place. There was also a selection of nineteenth-century tomes on Egyptian history.

'I served there briefly, you know.'

Eric turned. He had not heard Colonel Delamere enter. The old man poured himself a cup of coffee. 'I was a young second lieutenant at the end of 1944. Served on the staff in Cairo . . . nothing derring-do with the Desert Rats, I'm afraid. But that's where I first came across Neil Scanlon. He was in the signals section. I suppose we became friendly because of his unerring ability to lay his hands on whisky and cigarettes.'

'I hadn't realised he'd served with you.'

'Oh, Neil is a man of parts,' Delamere remarked drily. 'But don't be put off by his cockiness. I'm not. I've put up with it for years, because he can be an entertaining companion . . . and a loyal friend.'

Eric listened politely as the old man began to reminisce about the times he had enjoyed with Scanlon in the Middle East and Europe. He explained they had lost touch for some years, drifted apart, until they had found themselves at the same function in the north-east, at which point they had renewed their friendship. They had become closer after the colonel's wife had died.

'Anyway,' he commented at last, 'it's really too bad of me to continue in this vein, after asking you if you'd be kind enough to have a chat with me. A matter of business, rather than an old man's reminiscing.' He drained his coffee cup. 'Perhaps you wouldn't mind coming up to my office, upstairs.'

As they made their way up the broad staircase, Delamere said over his shoulder, 'Young Felshaw and that charming Miss Castle are leaving shortly, I believe. You don't wish to see them before they go?'

'I've already said goodbye to Miss Castle.'

'No doubt,' Delamere smiled. 'And Anne?'

'I don't need to see her. I'll probably call in at Sedleigh Hall this afternoon, on the way back.'

'Then we have an hour to ourselves.'

Eric followed the colonel along the first floor corridor until they reached a door which was locked. Delamere fumbled with a key, unlocked the door and stood aside, gesturing to Eric to enter. He was surprised by what met his gaze. Against one wall stood a mahogany desk with leather inlay, somewhat worn and faded. There was a laptop computer on the desk, a few files stacked neatly beside it, but the rest of the room was taken up with glass-fronted display cases filed with various mementoes of the colonel's past. They ranged from medals and other war memorabilia, including some framed citations, to objects of bronze and wood, obtained in various parts of the world — India, Malaysia, China, South Africa, Egypt.

'I am, I fear, a man of a collective disposition,' Colonel Delamere sighed. 'Which is one of the reasons why I wish to talk with you.' He paused, eyeing one particular piece in the display case. It was made of wood, in the form of a crouching man with the head of what appeared to be a jackal. He stood in front of it for a few seconds, thoughtfully.

'Egyptian?' Eric queried, breaking into the old man's reverie.

Delamere nodded. 'Anubis. The Guardian of the Dead.' He sighed, turned away, seated himself at his desk and gestured to Eric to take a seat himself, facing his host. 'And talk of the dead we must.'

'Sir?'

Delamere hesitated, fixed Eric with a worried frown and then half turned, opened the drawer of his desk and took out a folder. 'This is a copy of my will,' he stated.

There was a short silence. Eric waited.

'It was drawn up some years ago by the senior partner in a firm at Morpeth, a man well known to me. He died recently. And the other members of the firm, *well,* if I say that they are inclined towards more exciting forms of business, corporate matters, high finance . . . perhaps you will know what I mean. More importantly, I don't *know* any of them.'

Eric hesitated. 'I'm not sure that's very important, Colonel. I mean, lawyers are much of a kind, they're bound by the same rules . . .'

'I've no doubt that's the case, young man,' Colonel Delamere interrupted, 'but I prefer that in matters of such . . . personal importance I can deal with someone in whom I have confidence.'

Eric stared at him. He had the crawling feeling that he had been right all along. His invitation to accompany Anne to Delamere Hall had been underpinned by motives other than those she had exposed.

'The fact is,' Colonel Delamere went on, 'I have been concerned by the sad loss of my legal friend. I've wanted to place my affairs in other hands than the Morpeth firm. And when I was talking to Anne a few weeks ago, she told me about you. A man of experience, she said. A man I could trust to carry out my wishes. A man of integrity.'

He eyed Eric soberly, caressing his sparse moustache with lean fingers. 'I still don't know you, of course, hut I like what I have seen. And I have Anne's recommendation. So I would like to ask you if you would agree to take over the administration of my estate.'

Eric's suspicions had been confirmed. This was Anne interfering again, albeit with the best of motives. It was her way, perhaps, of nudging him back into a circle of acquaintances of consequence, connections of importance, a way of dragging his practice up to the level that she considered it should belong. No doubt Susie Cartwright would approve. Eric wasn't so sure he did.

'I'm flattered, Colonel, but I don't see—'

'It's neither an onerous task, nor a particularly lucrative one,' the old man assured him. 'Little needs to be done until I die, of course. My will does not need changing, other than for the naming of a new executor. You, if you agree. The bequests I make, the legacies I mention, these can all stand. And I'm not ill, or anything like that. I've no intention of joining my ancestors just yet. But I feel I need someone I can trust.'

'If it's all so straightforward,' Eric demurred, 'I don't see why you need to place such special emphasis upon—'

'Mr Ward . . . may I call you Eric? The reality is, while most of my estate is easily dealt with when the time comes . . .' His eyes strayed to his collection of memorabilia. 'The items there, for instance, most will go to the museum at Newcastle as I've already arranged . . .' His glance flicked back to Eric, his eyes hooding strangely, suddenly evasive. 'But there is one task I will need my executor to deal with, which is . . . a little delicate, in my view.'

Eric frowned, unsure how to react. A small knot of resentment still burnt in his chest, but he felt himself weakening. This was not going to be a major change in his life, or a return to the old days. He was not unwilling to help the old man, if the colonel felt he was the right person to handle his estate.

'Some months ago I reached a decision,' Colonel Delamere announced. 'I wrote a letter to the Foreign Office, regarding certain issues which I thought were of importance. I received a brief acknowledgment of my communication, but nothing more. Now it may be that my . . . anxieties are groundless, but nevertheless, I must feel sure that the right thing will be done, when the time comes. As it is, I feel I've waited too long, that this should have been dealt with a long time ago . . . but, as I say, a collector at heart . . . It is difficult to ignore the pattern of a lifetime.'

'So what is it you would want of your executor?' Eric asked, puzzled.

There was a short silence. Colonel Delamere looked at his hands; the skin was almost transparent, the veins and sinews standing out, the brown age spots showing blotchy against the pale background. 'It may be,' the colonel continued, 'that I attach too much importance to the matter. On the other hand, it could be that some lowly clerk in the Foreign Office did not have the wit or intelligence to see how important . . .' He fell into a brief reverie again, as Eric waited.

Colonel Delamere shook himself. 'I am certain, personally, the matter is important. Consequently, if you agree to take on the executorship of my estate we will check the details of my will again. But the main thing I need your word on is, in the event of my death, you will send to the Under-Secretary for Foreign Affairs in the Foreign Office the sealed letter that you will find locked in the safe there, in the corner of this room.'

'You just want me to send a letter?' Eric asked.

The old man nodded slowly. 'The letter only. And after that, you will receive a request. From the Foreign Office. The matter is fully explained in the sealed instructions that will be available to you, in the event of my death.' He permitted himself a wintry smile. 'Which I trust will be a circumstance we shall not be visiting in the too near future.' He eyed Eric steadily. 'Not too onerous a task, I'm sure you'll agree?'

Eric hesitated, then nodded. As far as he could see, acting as Delamere's executor was unlikely to eat too deeply into his principles . . .

CHAPTER 2

Charlie Spate was in love.

At least, he thought that maybe he was in love.

That was the whole point, he considered sourly as he stood staring out across the Jarrow buildings to the skeletal arms of the cranes, stark against the sky beyond the south shore cruise terminal. It was the uncertainty of it all.

When he and Elaine Start were in bed together he was confident, not just in the way that she aroused him, but in the passions that he seemed to inspire in her. She could be like an animal in bed, wild, demanding, exhausting. She awoke deep feelings in him, unleashing desires he had rarely if ever experienced before. And he had been with some practised women, in the old days, in the Met. Women who demonstrated passion for a purpose: financial gain.

But the problem was that away from her home, back working together she kept her distance. She was cool, aloof, controlled in a way he resented. Charlie would have liked more recognition of their personal relationship — the occasional caress of her buttock in a quiet corner, a snatched cuddle in the car. Of course, such behaviour would in the end be noticed by others at headquarters — it was never possible to keep an affair quiet in such circumstances. But for

Charlie that was part of the whole excitement of the thing: the furtive stroking, the knowledge that he and Elaine Start had a secret relationship that others for the moment had no suspicion of . . .

But that wasn't a game Detective Sergeant Elaine Start played. At work she was constrained, kept him at arm's length verbally as well as physically.

And it irritated him. It made him uncertain of his situation. And it also made him short-tempered.

So he put it down to love.

She was like that even now, as they sat together in the office in the tower block, looking out over Jarrow and the hills of County Durham, and the dark blue streak of the Tyne, winding its way out to sea. Cool, quiet, almost demure. Bloody hell, he thought savagely, demure was something you could never call Elaine Start. Not when you caught her in a darkened room, naked, letting herself go . . . He wriggled uncomfortably, his body moving distractingly at the memories . . .

'Where the hell is this guy?' he snapped irritably.

Elaine picked up the cup of coffee from the tray and drained it. She set it down again, not looking at him. She shrugged. 'You heard what his secretary said. Ten minutes.'

'This is police business,' Charlie snarled. 'And he seems to forget it's all for his benefit.'

'Ah, relax a bit, Charlie,' said Detective Sergeant Macmillan, leaning back in his chair on the other side of the room. 'Take the weight off your feet for a while. We do enough chasing around as it is. Ten minutes here or there, what's the difference?'

Charlie scowled at him. He didn't approve of Sam Macmillan having been put in charge of liaison on this business. For that matter he didn't much approve of Macmillan in any sense. The guy had cocked things up over that Fisher business — after all, it was all simple procedure, keep the forensic stuff bagged, make sure it didn't come into contact with other specimens, and label the stuff clearly for the labs.

And the bloody fool Macmillan had blown the thing, made a fool of himself, and the forensic team hadn't helped either. Fisher had walked. Thanks to that bastard Ward. Aided by police incompetence.

As for the liaison itself — Charlie wasn't at all sure why they'd been dragged from Northumberland into this business. The attacks on Blanding and Jacobs, Shipping Agents, had been at their offices in Jarrow, south of the Tyne, out of Charlie's jurisdiction. But Assistant Chief Constable Charteris called the shots, the smooth bastard. 'I'm assigning you to work a while south of the river, on a fire-bombing case. Chief wants an overall view. So you work with the South Tyneside people.'

'Why—'

'Need-to-know basis at the moment, and you don't need to know.' Charteris stared him down, challenging him to argue. 'It's a decision from the top. You can use DS Start, as usual. And DS Macmillan will be undertaking the liaison work.'

Smooth bastard. Charlie's glance slipped to Elaine, seated calmly, ignoring him. Charteris would be itching to get inside her knickers, Charlie knew. Had been for ages. No chance with Charlie Spate around. Unless . . .

Christ, he must be in love.

With a sense of relief he heard the door open. He turned to face the man they had come to see. Business type. Smooth, controlled face, confident. Charlie disliked him on sight. Too successful. Too organised. Too arrogant.

'Mr Felshaw?' Charlie said. 'We've been waiting—'

Felshaw interrupted him with a flashing, insincere smile. 'I'm sorry. Business meeting detained me. My secretary looked after you, I'm sure.' He moved smoothly behind the wide rosewood desk, and slipped into the leather chair. He placed elegant hands on the desk top, looked at each of his visitors in turn. Elaine smiled faintly. Macmillan sat up, a little more upright. Charlie remained standing. Irritated.

'So,' Felshaw said slowly, 'Are we any further on in the investigation?'

'Progress has been made, Mr Felshaw,' Macmillan replied before Charlie could speak.

'Which is why you'll be here, I imagine. Not that I'm fully convinced the matter needs such . . . emphasis. A few minor attacks, nothing our own security couldn't handle—'

'That's not quite the way our people see it. *Sir.*' Charlie made no attempt to keep the dislike out of his tone.

Felshaw looked at him steadily. 'That's as may be. But all these interviews, all this interruption to our business . . . I'm not at all certain it's worth it, in the end. Things like this happen, they die down of their own accord. Disaffected employees—'

'No. Not employees,' Charlie interrupted him. 'We've come to the conclusion that we can clear the people you named as having been involved. Our own investigations, together with our colleagues from South Tyneside now lead us to believe the attacks were orchestrated by a local group, based in South Shields. The local force is looking into it.'

Felshaw bared his teeth thoughtfully. He looked down at his hands, spread his fingers wide. 'A local group . . . with what motives?'

'That's something we have yet to determine,' DS Macmillan intervened. 'But we think it may be political. Disaffected youth, wanting to make a statement about their own position, second-class citizens in society . . .'

There was a short silence. Felshaw shook his head in doubt. 'I fail to see the significance, attacking our shipping agency, I mean. But if you've identified the group, I suppose you can now do something about it all. Bring them to justice.'

Elaine Start cleared her throat. She looked up at Felshaw, as he regarded her dispassionately. A cold man, Charlie considered, if he could look at her and see only a police officer. That bosom, and those legs . . .

'The fact is, sir,' Elaine commented, 'the two people we're pretty certain carried out the attacks — sending the rather amateur firebombs, in particular — well, they're aged thirteen and fifteen.'

Felshaw raised his eyebrows. 'You mean this is all just a simple prank?'

'You can be a villain even if you're under age,' Charlie snapped. 'And these kids are dangerous.'

'Have you heard of a group called the Sand Dancers?' Elaine continued, flashing a warning glance at Charlie, as though she was in charge of this business, rather than he.

Felshaw gave a short bark of a laugh, dismissively. 'You're joking. The term is a derogatory one, applied generally by local people to Yemeni immigrants. Even to the Yemeni who have been here for three generations. I'm surprised to hear you use the term.'

Elaine Start could be stubborn, Charlie knew. He saw her raise her chin, perceived the glitter in her eye. 'I'm aware of the use of the term, sir. But I should point out it's one they use themselves, in this case. A matter of self-mockery, I suspect. But be that as it may, the fact is these two boys were not working alone. We believe they are merely the fringe of a more solid organisation — young people out to prove themselves. What they've probably done was not with the approval of the men more closely bound to the centre of the group. However, we can't be sure.' She glanced at Charlie. He took the hint.

'What we'd like to do, Mr Felshaw, is extend our enquiries somewhat. We know there is an organisation called the Sand Dancers, and we've been given some leads . . .' He gritted his teeth: Charteris hadn't told him where the leads came from. 'To follow them up we'll need your agreement to inspect your employment records. And the contracts with the firms you deal with.'

Felshaw's mouth tightened. He stared at Charlie with narrowed eyes. 'Why would you want to do that?'

'These boys have been influenced by older youths and men. We want to trace the employment records of people we've been able to put names to. They, in turn, have probably made contacts with people working with the companies who have contracted with you. By using such information—'

'Detective Chief Inspector,' Felshaw interrupted, with an ominous note in his voice. 'Some of the companies who deal with us are very large operations. They are based in Holland, Nassau, Norway, South Africa . . . they have multinational connections. Are you seriously suggesting that I should hand over confidential information to you without their permission?'

Charlie Spate shrugged. 'How you deal with the matter is naturally up to you, sir, but if we can get—'

Felshaw held up an admonitory hand. 'Let's just hold it there, Mr Spate. There's no way I can allow you access to these details.'

'You've been fire-bombed—'

'By a couple of children,' Felshaw sneered. 'Kids out on the rampage, playing at big men, hoping to impress their elders. They did no damage of any consequence, I remind you. If you know the names of these youngsters all right, put them in front of the juvenile court, scare the hell out of them — but don't expect me to take it so seriously that I run the risk of jeopardising my own operations.' He folded his arms in front of him, held Charlie's glance. 'My board of directors wouldn't thank me for it. In fact, they'd probably sack me.'

'Mr Felshaw—'

'I don't think there's anything you can say which will make me change my mind,' the shipping agent interrupted. 'What you ask is impossible. It would cause too much disruption. It could give rise to rumours among employees. Confidential information on people and contracts would be laid bare — and no one would thank me for it. Certainly not my directors. And when the police come up with nothing useful — as I think would be the case — I would be the one hung out to dry. I'm sorry, Mr Spate. I can't agree to your request. Put the fear of Allah into these kids — if they are Yemenis — but don't involve the firm of Blanding and Jacobs any further.'

Charlie was about to argue, but Felshaw was rising to his feet. 'I'm sorry but I'll have to ask you to leave now. I have business to transact.'

'These attacks could be just the beginning of something—'

'Then I'm sure you'll do all in your power to act if the situation changes. But first, put these kids in a remand home or something. And leave me to get on with my job.'

The three police officers left, stiff-backed. Macmillan stood by his car. 'You'll make the report back at Ponteland?' he asked. 'I'd better go and report to the South Tyneside guys.'

And find a nice quiet pub where you can relax for a few hours, Charlie thought savagely. But he said nothing, nodded his head, and slipped into the passenger seat beside Elaine Start.

When she drove the car out of the yard he was tempted to put his hand on her thigh, but he thought better of it.

Love could be a bloody worrying experience. In some ways, lust was better. That was the way it used to be. He swore under his breath as they headed for the Tyne Tunnel to take the A19 north towards the airport, and headquarters at Ponteland.

* * *

They had made their way to Ponteland almost in silence, both preoccupied with their own thoughts. It was only when they pulled into the car park outside headquarters that Elaine asked, 'Do you think Felshaw was talking straight with us?'

'How do you mean?'

'That guff about protecting his confidential business information, and the board of directors not understanding. It seemed to me he had some other agenda on his mind.'

'Such as?'

'Hell, I don't know. It's just that he didn't sound convincing to me.'

Charlie sighed. He had known many men in the Met who would clam up if anyone tried to delve into their books. 'These guys, they never like to have the police snooping around. Maybe Felshaw's got something to hide. Maybe he hasn't. I think it's just he's afraid to open up to us just in case something unpleasant does emerge. How the hell do I know? Maybe he's on the fiddle. Maybe he's got some dicey dealings out there on the high seas. I'm sick of the thing anyway. Chasing kids with half-cooked firebombs. I've got far better things to do with my time.'

'You going to tell Charteris that?' Elaine asked, eyeing him disbelievingly.

There was a subtle challenge in her tone. He knew she suspected his feelings towards the assistant chief constable were soured in part by the clear admiration Charteris had for her. The hell with it, he thought, not answering her. He got out of the car. 'Get an appointment with the ACC this afternoon. We need to let him know that this chicken ain't going to run.'

Charlie made his way back to his office, glowered at the paperwork on his desk, locked the door behind him and opened the drawer of his desk. He took out the half-empty bottle of Scotch, fished a paper cup from the same drawer, and poured himself a hefty slug. He stared at the ceiling and shook his head. There were times when he wished he was still at the Met. Life had seemed somehow less complicated down there. Plenty of villains; more than enough skulduggery to deal with; a bit of muscle to terrify — and as much skirt as a man could want. Life up here . . . He tilted the paper cup, let the hot spirit bite at the back of his throat.

He was still sitting there half an hour later when the phone rang. It was Elaine Start.

'He wants to see us at three-thirty.'

'You drop him a hint that all is not well with his pet project?' Charlie sneered. 'Chasing little kids up alleys?'

She was silent for a few seconds. He detected disapproval in the silence. 'I told him we had hit some problems.

He didn't seem too much bothered, as it happened. I think he's got something else he wants us to attend to.'

'Let's hope it's not wiping his arse for him.' The phone went dead abruptly.

* * *

Assistant Chief Constable Jim Charteris was in a strange mood. Charlie knew it as soon as he and Elaine entered the office. Charlie didn't like Charteris: he thought he was a smooth, ambitious bastard whose first duty was to himself: he had his eyes set on a passage to the top, away from this force. He was always immaculately uniformed, his greying hair slicked back neatly, his eyes slightly hooded, a frown of concentration on his face to demonstrate to people that he was always listening, calculating, on top of his job. But today there was something else about him: his handsome features were set grimly, his lips tighter than normal, and he barely gave Elaine Start a glance as she came in.

That was unusual in itself. Like Charlie, he had always seemed appreciative of her bosom.

Charlie thought it best to go straight into the attack. 'We had the meeting with Felshaw at Blanding and Jacobs this morning, sir. It was unproductive. He refuses to cooperate. We weren't able to agree why that should be, though DS Start and I haven't yet had time to sit down properly and compare notes . . .'

'What?'

It was as though Charteris hadn't been listening. His face was blank, his mouth angry.

'I was saying, sir . . . the enquiry into those kids who sent packages to Blanding and Jacobs—'

'You can leave that for now,' Charteris snapped. He rose from behind his desk and began to prowl around the room like an angry bear. 'There's been a break-in. A burglary.' Charlie widened his eyes and glanced at Elaine. She also seemed surprised.

'You two had better get on to it.'

'Sir?' Charlie was surprised, but his surprise was turning to anger. He had been set on this stupid business in Jarrow — outside his force's jurisdiction — and it was proving to be kid's stuff, with an uncooperative victim to boot and now he was being told to forget it and get on with a burglary! What the hell was going on? 'A burglary, sir? Whose house was it, the Chief Constable's?'

Charteris didn't like the crack. When he swivelled his head to glare at Charlie his eyes were cold. 'It's about time you learnt, DCI Spate, that things up here are different from what you got up to in the Met. Up here, you follow orders, and you do it without giving off at the mouth.'

For a moment Charlie was about to make an angry response but he stopped himself, suddenly aware that Charteris was really niggled about something. His anger was not essentially directed at Charlie: it had some other source. It was as though he had been told to do something that he was unwilling to do.

'What's so special about this burglary, sir?' Elaine Start asked. 'I mean, it's not the kind of thing you'd normally expect to put two officers of our rank onto. I mean, the uniformed—'

'It's up in the county. Delamere Hall.'

Charlie groaned mentally. It was an old boys' network issue. Some wealthy landowner had got his best knickknacks lifted, rung up the Chief Constable, and off the cavalry would ride into the hills, making a great show, achieving little but showing the great and the good that they still had a direct line to their old chum, the Chief Constable.

'Surely, sir, the Chief can satisfy his old muckers in the county by arranging for a couple of coppers to get up there and—'

'You're a couple of coppers,' Charteris snarled. 'Besides, this isn't the Old Man's doing.'

Puzzled, Charlie glanced at Elaine Start. 'I don't understand . . .' he began.

Assistant Constable Jim Charteris glared at him, thumped his fist on the desk top and recommenced his pacing of the room. 'Don't feel yourself badly let down, Spate, by being given a minor break-in to deal with. You're not alone. I'm in charge of scarce resources, and now I'm asked . . . I'm *ordered* to give this matter a high priority. Why, for God's sake? Things are falling apart around here, I can tell you that! First this bloody enquiry south of the river, which turns out to be a couple of kids. Now it's a bloody burglary in Northumberland at which I'm supposed to throw one of my senior officers! And when I ask why, all I get is platitudinous crap! You're upset, Spate? For God's sake, so am I!'

Charlie Spate was speechless. The tirade was unexpected; indeed, it was unprecedented. Charteris was a career-minded officer: he was looking for a quick ride to the top. He was not the kind of man who would start rocking boats. Nor would he normally even think of sounding off to officers below him in rank.

Something had needled him, got under his skin.

Charlie was unprepared to push things any further. This all needed thinking about. 'Delamere Hall,' he muttered.

'That's right. North of Ogle. Out in the bloody hills somewhere. A burglary. Quite a lot of damage, it seems. And the owner: he's ended up in hospital. Could be serious. But what the bloody hell . . .'

His voice died away. The seething rage which had been consuming him began to fade. He felt more in control of himself. He swallowed hard and returned to sit down behind his desk. 'You drop everything else. You investigate this break-in. You make an inventory of all that's missing.'

He spread his fingers wide on the desktop. He hunched his shoulders. There was a sneer on his handsome features. 'And you report directly to me. That's what it comes down to these days, it seems. You two drop anything else you're involved in — you leave the South Tyneside enquiry to Macmillan — and you report directly to me.' He shook his head. 'A burglary. What the hell is the world coming to!'

65

For almost the first time in their acquaintance, Charlie was in agreement with the assistant chief constable.

* * *

Almost two weeks had passed since Eric had first met Colonel Jock Delamere, at the weekend at Delamere Hall. Time had passed swiftly: he had been busy with an attempted rape at Benton, a fraudulent trading case up at Alnwick — which in terms of location at least was a pleasant change from Newcastle villainy — and had been busy drawing up some haulage contracts for a company in Byker, who were just starting out on a lucrative business of moving furniture for one of the big stores operating throughout the north-east. He hoped it wasn't a cover for something more nefarious, such as smuggled cigarettes from France, or fake Ecstasy tablets from the Netherlands. You could never tell these days.

He had been tempted several times to make contact with Sarah Castle, for he found her attractive. And he thought he had detected a spark of interest in her eyes. On the other hand she had been fairly firm when he had suggested they meet again: she said she would contact him. She had not done so: that was probably the end of the matter, he thought philosophically.

In spite of his busy schedule he had nevertheless found time to make another visit to Delamere Hall, having finally decided to act as the old man's executor. Jock Delamere had entertained him to lunch, and they had spent the afternoon going over details of his possessions. They had discussed the legacies he had decided upon — they were mainly to charitable bodies, since the colonel seemed to have no living relatives. 'My wife and I,' he had said sadly, 'we did have one son but he was killed in a skiing accident in Austria. As for other family . . . I've no doubt there are some distant cousins, but none that I'm aware of. The family never really kept in touch, I suppose. And I was away in the Middle East for many years. Along with Neil Scanlon.'

They had gone to his locked office and together had drawn up an inventory of the items that he kept in his collection. Eric formed the view that some of them would be quite valuable, and would be seen as welcome additions to the museum in Newcastle under the terms of the will Delamere had signed. The colonel took some of the items down from the display cases as he talked about them: some of them were trivial items retained for their nostalgic connections; others had been picked up in various antique shops around the world. A number of items were clearly of some value, if they were original pieces, which Eric suspected they were. They varied from items of wood, to bronze and some small gold objects. Delamere handled them all proudly. They were his past.

While Eric made up the list, amended since it had been worked on by the previous firm of Morpeth solicitors, Delamere had placed the Anubis artefact, that Eric had noticed in the display case previously, on the desk beside him. He sat there now, his left hand slowly stroking the polished ebony surface. The head was masked with bronze, the ears tipped with gold, and the eyes were of lapis lazuli. Delamere seemed to regard it with a certain respect.

'I don't see the jackal head on your list, Colonel,' Eric mentioned. 'It looks like a valuable item — do you have any other plans for it? It will need to be included if I'm to act as your executor.'

Delamere hesitated for several moments. He gazed at the figure as though distracted, caught up in his thoughts. Slowly, he shook his head. 'No, don't include it in the list of bequests to the museum. I haven't yet quite decided on its future. Much will depend . . .' He fell silent, reflective, a frown on his brow.

They said no more about it. It was Delamere's business, after all.

'Now, this other matter you mentioned to me,' Eric said. The letter to the Foreign Office.'

The colonel still seemed a little distracted, but after a moment he nodded. He rose, locked the display case, leaving the jackal-headed figurine on the desk. 'The letter . . .' he murmured. 'Yes, I'm in the process of rewriting it, so many things to think about. However, I shall be placing the letter in that safe over there, as I explained to you. Along with it shall be detailed instructions to you, as executor, which will go some way to explaining what I want finally settled in relation to my estate. Now, the combination to the safe . . .' He frowned, scratched his lean cheek, fiddled with his sparse moustache. 'Rather than burden you with it just now, I have left the combination in a deposit box in my bank in Morpeth. After my death, armed with the copy of my will which you will have for safe keeping, you will be able to obtain the combination — I have already instructed the bank in this respect — and carry out my last wishes . . .'

When the inventory was finally completed, Eric said he would take it back with him to the office, send Delamere a copy for his own files, and retain a copy himself to be added to the will. They finished their business in the drawing room over a glass of whisky, while Delamere enjoyed a Havana cigar. It was, he explained to Eric, a rare treat. The more enjoyable since he had been warned off such activity by his doctor.

Apart from his slightly distracted air that day, Colonel Delamere had seemed in good health, and in good spirits. Accordingly, Eric was unprepared for the phone call he received from Anne a week later.

'Eric, it's terrible news.' Her voice seemed strangled, as she struggled with her emotions.

'What's the matter? What's happened?'

'It's Jock Delamere. There was a burglary at the Hall last night. I don't know what happened precisely, but it seems someone broke in during the early hours of the morning. Jock must have heard the intruders, came down the stairs with a walking stick — he sleeps on the second floor — and challenged them. He should never have tried . . . he should have called the police . . . They beat him rather badly.'

'Where is he now?' Eric asked.

'He's been taken to hospital in Newcastle. The poor man! I hope he's going to be all right. But at his age—'

'He was pretty fit, Anne. Don't worry too much about it,' he attempted to assure her. 'He'll be all right. You've not been to see him?'

'It's not been possible. But I'm hoping to go this afternoon. He's been in intensive care and—'

'I'll meet you there,' Eric assured her. 'I should be through in court by about three. I'll see you there, at the hospital.'

He met her in the vestibule. She was seated in the small cafe set up for waiting visitors. She stood up, came to greet him as he entered. She explained that she had not been allowed access to the old man. He was still in intensive care.

Eric took her arm. 'Let's go see what's happening.'

He explained to the girl in reception that he was the colonel's solicitor. She made a phone call, and in a little while they were led along the corridor to a private ward. There was a police constable seated outside the ward: a gloomy-looking young doctor emerging from the room spoke briefly to him. Eric was surprised at the police presence. He guessed that the officer would be there either for the old man's further protection, or because it was felt they needed to get information from him as quickly as possible. It was a somewhat unusual procedure. Perhaps Colonel Delamere had friends in high places.

The doctor came forward to meet them as they stood outside the ward. 'I understand you wanted to see Colonel Delamere.'

'We came to see if he was all right,' Anne said quickly. 'Maybe have a word with him—'

'That won't be easy,' the young doctor with the mournful spaniel eyes informed them. 'Colonel Delamere has been badly beaten. I won't bother you with the medical condition in detail, but he's suffered severe injuries to his head, and he's not a young man. We're more than a little concerned about his condition, and we certainly can't allow access to him. You're not family, I take it?'

Eric shook his head. 'No. A friend . . . and I'm his legal representative.'

The surgeon shook his head. 'I see. Well, I hope I'm wrong, but I'm not at all sanguine about his chances of coming out of this attack . . . undamaged, shall we say? He's in a coma, he has difficulty breathing . . . but we're monitoring him constantly. I'm afraid that's as much as I can say at the moment.'

There was little they could do. They left the hospital and went out to the car park. Standing beside her car, Anne said, 'I'm so sad about all this. I hope he pulls through. He and my father were good friends . . .' She paused, then glanced up at Eric. 'So you took up his request, then? To act as his lawyer.'

'Which you had set up,' Eric muttered.

'It was not so much for *you*,' Anne argued. 'The colonel was worried; things have been getting him down for some reason. And he told me he wanted someone he could trust, someone who could take pressure, stay loyal . . .' She held his glance, stubbornly. 'You're the best lawyer I know, Eric, even if you do waste your time and talents on the Quayside.'

There was a certain defiance in her tone. Eric put a hand on her arm, soothingly. 'It's all right. I know you were acting out of the best motives. I'm pleased that you recommended me. I just hope that my services as an executor won't be called upon too soon.'

'Eric, you don't think—'

Her voice died away, the anxious words recalled. He was silent for a while, just holding her hand. She was clearly distressed. 'What are you going to do now?' she asked at last.

He shrugged. 'I suppose I'd better get up to Delamere Hall, check out what damage has been done, what's been taken in the robbery. I've got an inventory that he and I had prepared. Then, I'd better make a report to the police.'

'They haven't been in touch?'

He shook his head. 'Wouldn't expect them to, not at this stage. They wouldn't even know I'm involved, I suppose. Anyway, leave things to me. I'll drive up there immediately, and see what needs to be done.' He checked his watch. 'I should be there in an hour. I'll give you a ring later, let you know what's happening.'

She nodded, kissed him lightly on the cheek and got into her car. As she drove away he stood there, looking after her. So much had happened over the years, since he had first seen her riding down through the woods on the hill, in the dappled sunshine. But at least they still remained friends . . .

* * *

When Eric turned off the main road and pulled the Celica into the drive leading to Delamere Hall he was not surprised to see a police car in front of the entrance. They would have been working at the scene of crime, and should be finishing about now. There was also a white van, which he guessed would belong to the forensic labs: as he parked his own car his guess was confirmed as he caught sight of two figures in white overalls emerging from the house. What did surprise him, however, was the sight of Detective Chief Inspector Charlie Spate standing on the steps.

He stood there with his arms folded, grim-visaged as Eric approached. 'Ward,' he drawled in a tone far from welcoming. 'So what bird of ill-omen brings you here? You taken to ambulance-chasing?'

Eric glanced around. There was another police car parked at the side of the house. They were taking this matter seriously, he thought. He ignored Spate's jibe. 'I wouldn't have thought this business warranted the presence of a DCI.'

'Things have changed since you left the force,' Spate snapped, as though Eric had touched a raw spot. 'And you haven't answered my question. What do you want here?'

'I'm Colonel Delamere's solicitor.'

Charlie Spate grimaced. 'Now is that so? Started going up in the world have you? Colonel Delamere, hey . . . bit different from your usual run of clients.'

Eric failed to rise to the bait. 'Can I go inside?'

'This is a police enquiry.'

'And I'm his legal representative. I need to see what's happened.'

'Why?'

Eric knew that Spate would be obstructive every step of the way. 'Let's put it like this, DCI. You're attending a burglary scene. You'll need to know at the very least what's been taken. Colonel Delamere — who would have been able to tell you — is in a coma. So, if you want to proceed sensibly in the business you need to find someone who can maybe give you a motive for the break-in.'

'Obvious.' Spate's tone was surly. 'Loot.'

'But you don't know what was actually taken. If anything. I can tell you.'

'How?' Spate demanded suspiciously.

'Because I made a full inventory of Delamere's possessions just a week ago. Now can I go inside?'

Spate didn't like it, but he saw the sense of letting Eric in. He stepped to one side. 'You can go in. But I'll be at your elbow, in case you lift anything yourself. And remember — this is a crime scene so keep your fingers off everything. I mean, if we picked up your DNA maybe we'd try to fit you up on this one.'

The sneer was not lost on Eric: he knew Spate was making veiled reference to the release of Joe Fisher.

With Spate at his back he went into the house. All appeared normal in the hallway. Over his shoulder, he asked, 'Was anyone else hurt in the attack?'

Spate grunted. 'There was only one other guy in the house. Some sort of butler. Hardly of the active type. But he sleeps at the back of the house and claims he was aware of nothing until he heard the old man shouting, there was a ruckus up on the first floor, and by the time he'd pulled himself together, got a dressing gown on — that sort of thing — and made his way up to the first floor, all he saw was Colonel Delamere lying in a pool of blood.'

'Where?'

'Outside the room he used as an office.'

Eric turned and frowned at the policeman. 'The office was open?'

'They forced the lock.'

'Why would burglars go for that room?'

Spate shrugged. 'Maybe they had inside information, maybe not. But if you was prowling around in the darkness, took a look in the downstairs rooms, then went up to the first floor, found a locked door, it wouldn't require the mind of a genius to work out that there might be something valuable behind there. So, they forced the lock. Maybe that was what woke the old man, on the floor above. That, or the sound of breaking glass when they smashed open the display cases.'

There was a white-coated figure emerging from the office. As Eric and Spate ascended the staircase, Spate called out. 'You all done?'

'Much as we can.'

'Took enough bloody time over it,' Spate complained.

Eric glanced at him curiously. Spate was clearly niggled about something, maybe upset about being involved in this business at all.

Eric walked ahead of him towards the room where he had earlier been seated with Delamere, going over the inventory. As soon as he entered he saw that the glass-fronted display cases had been smashed; shards of glass littered the floor. He stepped carefully past them, edging towards the desk, careful to touch nothing. The desk had been broken open: splinters of wood stood up from the broken lock.

'Jemmied open,' Spate said indifferently 'Cleared it out on the floor. Nothing special left there, we can see.'

Eric couldn't recall seeing the colonel open that drawer. 'Did he keep the inventory there?'

'Not that we've found,' Spate replied.

'It's probably in the safe,' Eric suggested.

'Not been opened,' Spate explained. 'Looks like that was too hard a nut for them to crack — either that, or Delamere disturbed them before they could have a go at it.'

'I have access to the combination. I can open it if needs be, but since it's not been cracked, nothing will have been taken from there, so I don't suppose its contents will be of interest to you.'

Spate eyed him suspiciously. 'You know we'll need to see anything that's relevant.'

'If it's still locked inside, it won't be relevant,' Eric insisted.

Spate let it go for the moment.

Eric looked back at the display cases: there was a jumble of artefacts lying scattered there, some on the floor.

'So you can tell us what's missing?' Spate demanded.

Eric shrugged. 'Not at a glance. Colonel Delamere was — is — a collector. All sorts of memorabilia, from his time in the Army, pieces he had picked up from around the world, some quite expensive stuff.'

'And you got a list.'

'At my office. I can let you have a copy later today.'

'Quicker the better, so we can start trawling around known fences. You know the drill.'

Eric nodded. He inspected the display case more closely. 'There are several things that seem to have gone. And . . . one thing I can certainly remember.'

'Something of value?'

Eric nodded. 'Considerable value, I would say.'

'What would that be?'

'A statuette. About a foot long, maybe. Made of ebony. Old. Probably very old. The wooden mask has been bronzed, there's some gold leaf on the head, the eyes are made of lapis lazuli. Head of a jackal. Anubis.'

Spate frowned. 'What the hell would that be?'

Eric looked at him. 'The Egyptians in ancient times believed in a large number of gods. They gave these gods animal forms: Osiris, a man-form with the head of a hawk, for instance. Anubis was another. He appeared in the form of a jackal. And he had a particular function.'

'And what might that have been?'

'He was the Keeper . . . the Guardian of the Dead.'

* * *

Sharon Owen declared she was free to join him for a light lunch for an hour or so. Accordingly, they arranged to meet at a restaurant, Prima's, at the lower end of Dean Street, close by Eric's own office and a short walk from Sharon's chambers. They found a table near the window overlooking the street itself: most of the early rush of businessmen and shoppers had eaten and left, so they were virtually alone in the section of the seating area that they had chosen. Sharon ordered a salad.

'Watching your figure?' Eric asked.

'Controlling it.'

She had little need to. In her dark business suit she looked smart, efficient and very attractive. He was still wondering whether he shouldn't be taking their relationship more seriously.

'So, to what do I owe the pleasure?' she asked as she sipped a glass of mineral water. 'It's not often you ask me out to lunch. Is this business or pleasure?'

'It's always a pleasure — but I wanted to raise a bit of business.'

'Talk to the clerk in chambers.' She pulled a face at him.

'He's not as pretty as you. Anyway he can wait. Until I've had a chat with you.' Eric hesitated, while he poured himself a glass of the white wine she had refused. 'You do much work these days for Bradley and Tindall?'

'Not me personally,' she replied, frowning slightly. 'They tend to use old Featherstone. Been giving him briefs for years.'

'What's he working on at the moment?' Eric asked innocently.

She shrugged. 'As far as I know, it's mainly immigration matters. Quite lucrative, I understand. Though come to think of it, he's been walking around with a face like a fiddle all morning, and he's had a long conference with the head of chambers. Something's put his nose out of joint.' She stared at Eric suspiciously. 'You're not thinking of briefing him are you? When you've far more attractive prospects in chambers, who have never let you down yet?'

Eric laughed. 'You and Joe Fisher, you mean.'

Her salad arrived, along with his fish. He leant forward. 'You sure you won't try some of this wine? No? Well, the thing is, Sharon, things have suddenly started looking up for me . . .'

He recalled the sight of Susie Cartwright's face as he had walked into the office that morning. She had a broad smile on her lips, and there was an air of triumph about her. She placed a hand on a thick box file on the desk in front of her. 'Well, Mr Ward, it looks as though you're going to build up your practice in spite of yourself. It's what I've been saying to you for years. You can do better than handle the cases you've been dealing with. And now, here it is, all handed to you on a plate.'

He stared at the box file, staying well away from it. 'So you're going to keep the good news a secret from me?'

She stood up, picked up the box file, forced it upon him with a flourish. 'We've finally vanquished the opposition. Bradley and Tindall.'

Eric grunted gloomily. 'Hardly opposition, Susie. Different league.'

It was a big firm in Newcastle, with branches in Sunderland and Middlesbrough. It enjoyed a solid if somewhat unadventurous reputation. Bradley and Tindall had twenty-two partners. They dealt with corporate clients, big firms, and wealthy clients. A considerable amount of National Health Service work came their way — they had three nominated partners — and they handled other lucrative contracts from government departments. They also had a shipping division, dealing with charters. They were big fish; he was a minnow. He eyed the file. He was curious. 'So what's this all about?'

Susie put her hands on her hips. She was a fine figure of a woman. There was a clerk in the Lord Chancellor's department who fancied her — since he dealt with court timetables it was a good contact to have. The odd favour came their way: the right judge, a useful timing . . .

'One of the legal executives came down this morning, from Bradley and Tindall. He brought this file: it's summary papers only. The rest of the stuff will be following later. There's a letter of explanation enclosed, it seems. But from what he told me his principals are not pleased. They've been instructed to hand over a load of work to you.'

Eric grimaced his surprise. 'I don't understand.'

'Are you going to argue with them about it? Talent will out, Mr Ward. Even if it's reluctant. It looks as though Bradley's have not been handling these Foreign Office briefs as they should have — and consequently it's all been dumped into your lap!'

Susie Cartwright had an uncomplicated view of the world. Eric was more suspicious: he was interested to discover just what lay behind this sudden gift. Perhaps there was one way he could find out . . .

Now, as he explained to Sharon Owen what had happened, she smiled. 'My God, no wonder old Featherstone was hopping about this morning. It's a slap in the eye for him — he's always been well in with Bradley's! And if they've lost a slice of business, it's going to affect him as well!'

'But why has it happened?' Eric asked. 'Have you heard anything on the grapevine?'

She shook her head, picked at her salad for a few moments and then shrugged. 'Not really. But I suppose I can ask around in chambers.' She glanced at him. 'So this is the reason why you asked me to lunch. I might have guessed. It's never anything to do with sex.' She grinned at him. 'Bit of a windfall for you though, Eric. Foreign Office briefs. That's where the big money comes in.'

'Secure money, anyway,' Eric suggested. 'But you know, I don't feel this is right. Gift horses—'

'Shouldn't get their teeth inspected too closely. Fact is, Eric, this is going to keep you pretty busy, small firm like yours.'

He laughed. 'I'll need a good barrister.'

'Like Featherstone?'

'As you said, there are others more attractive.'

She giggled. 'So I'll get something more than lunch out of this. Mind you, it'll cause steam to rise in chambers . . . But, there you are. Fact is, my friend, you seem to be rising in the legal world.' She paused. 'I hear you're handling the estate of Colonel Delamere too.'

'News travels.'

'The legal world: all networks. That was a bad business at Delamere. The break-in, and his death later. Any problems with the estate?'

Eric shook his head. 'Not really. Pretty straightforward really. Except that a number of the items he's bequeathed are missing of course, stolen in the burglary.'

And there was the matter of the curious request disclosed in the letter of instructions Eric had finally retrieved from the safe, after obtaining the combination from the bank. But that was not a matter he should be discussing with Sharon . . .

* * *

The letter had been written a week or so before the break-in, after Eric had agreed to handle the estate. The main part of the letter was standard enough, explaining what Delamere intended by way of the bequests mentioned in the will. He had been a meticulous man: dotting and crossing in all the relevant places. The last few paragraphs were more difficult to understand.

'Lastly, I come to the matter of the sealed letter which I wish you to send to the Under-Secretary for Foreign Affairs, at the Foreign Office. I should explain that I wrote to them some time ago but apart from a brief acknowledgment heard nothing more. I cannot believe that the Foreign Office has misunderstood what I had to say, but, unless the matter is settled before my decease, I wish you to send the sealed letter kept in my safe.

'The likely result will be that a member of the Foreign Office will then contact you in the capacity of my executor. The individual will produce the sealed letter that you will have sent them, and after taking appropriate safeguards regarding identity and so forth — which I leave to your good judgment — you will place in the hands of the Foreign Office representative the statuette of the jackal-headed Anubis which you have already seen among my possessions.

'In the unlikely event that you receive no visit from a Foreign Office official, you will proceed to London and request an interview with a senior official of that office to whom you will then hand the Anubis figure. I stress that this matter is of importance, and your discretion must be applied at all times . . .'

The problem was, of course, that as a consequence of the break-in, the Anubis statuette had disappeared. While it was no longer possible for Eric to follow the instructions completely, he had nevertheless decided that the sealed letter at least should be sent to London, as Colonel Delamere had demanded.

Since then, there had been silence.

Until somewhat mysteriously a package of briefs regarding immigration cases had been dropped into his lap. Bradley and Tindall were spitting blood, no doubt, but that was nothing to do with him. But he still waited for an explanation.

It came two days later.

Susie Cartwright came into his office with a surprised look on her face. 'There's a gentleman wishes to make an appointment. For this morning if possible. He says he's from the Foreign Office. Do you think it's in connection with the cases that Bradley and Tindall have handed over?'

Eric would have bet money on it.

The man from the Foreign Office introduced himself as Charles Linwood-Forster. He was perhaps fifty years of age, beak-nosed, lean, slight of build and careful of manner. He had the eyes of a patient owl, suggesting to the world that he had seen everything and could be amazed by nothing. He was dressed in a dark grey, pin-striped suit. To Eric's surprise he carried neither a bowler hat nor an umbrella. It appeared that he had adopted different practices from normal for his trip to the north.

At least he hadn't adopted a cloth cap.

Eric shook hands with him: the handshake gave nothing away. He waved Linwood-Forster to a seat and settled down behind his desk. He raised an interrogative eyebrow. 'I imagine your visit will have something to do with the briefs that have been transferred to me by the firm of Bradley and Tindall.'

Linwood-Forster permitted himself a thin smile, and crossed his legs, flicking away at the knee as though discarding fluff. 'I thought it would be appropriate to discuss them in person.'

'I was surprised to see them.'

'You need not be surprised. You are regarded in the department as a man of conviction, perspicacity . . . and integrity.'

'Now I'm worried as well as surprised.'

'There was an explanatory letter, was there not!'

'There was indeed. But it did little to overcome my surprise. This is a small firm, Bradley and Tindall are big hitters—'

'Ah, yes, well there's the rub, you see, Mr Ward.' Linwood-Forster sat very straight in his chair, fingers linked together in his lap. 'There's been a certain change of policy in the Ministry. There's a feeling among our political masters that the work we're involved in should be spread around. In delicate matters such as immigration, the department has been under attack, arguments about speed of action, that sort of thing, and it's been felt that it would help if the work were . . . more dispersed, shall we say!'

'To smaller firms!' Eric queried, disbelievingly.

'With fewer resources, admittedly . . . but then, a firm like yours would naturally give a higher priority to the business.' Linwood-Forster sniffed, looked around the room. No doubt he felt it appeared shabby. Undeterred, he went on, 'In any event, our political masters have so decreed, we have acted, and we are expecting favourable results from your attention to these cases.'

'I thought immigration matters fell within the purview of the Home Office,' Eric remarked.

The thin smile came back, wary at the edges. 'Not completely.'

He vouchsafed no further information. After a short silence he moved on to another topic, and Eric began to understand.

'This could be the commencement of an important period in your legal life, Mr Ward.' Linwood-Forster's smile was thin; he flicked out a lizard-like tongue, and with his left hand picked at the sleeve of his jacket. Eric saw nothing there. He waited.

'I'm sure other retainers will come your way,' the civil servant continued, 'from time to time, in spite of your running such a small operation. But it will be in recognition of your discretion, as much as anything else.' His pale eyes regarded Eric coldly. 'In all matters that might affect the government.'

'You're buying my silence,' Eric guessed.

'Come my dear sir, nothing so crude. Naturally, acting as you now are on behalf of the Foreign Office in several transactions, you will be regarded as the custodian of client information and you will need to observe the usual . . . loyalties to your client.' He paused, eyeing Eric with a casual indifference. 'I understand you were also recently appointed to act as the executor in the matter of the estate of the late lamented Colonel Delamere. A gentleman well known to us of late. In the capacity of executor you have had need to contact the Foreign Office.'

'Those were Colonel Delamere's instructions.'

'Indeed. And those instructions were to accede to the wishes of the Foreign Office in the disposal of . . . a certain object.'

'That's true.' He paused. 'When a copy of the letter the colonel sent to London was shown to me.'

'Ah . . .' Linwood-Forster smiled thinly, put his left hand inside his jacket and produced an envelope. It was addressed to the Under-Secretary for Foreign Affairs. He opened the envelope, showed Eric the letter. He was careful to disclose nothing of its contents other than the signature of the dead man. 'This is what you mean?'

'It seems so.' Eric nodded, waiting. 'What's this got to do with the briefs I've received?'

'My dear boy, nothing, I assure you, nothing at all. Separate issues, believe me. But since I was visiting, it seemed the appropriate moment . . . Did you ever have much opportunity to inspect the object in question?'

'The Anubis statuette?' Eric nodded. 'I saw it briefly. A couple of times, actually. I didn't handle it, or look at it very closely.'

'Hmmm.' Linwood-Forster seemed slightly disturbed by Eric's identifying the object referred to in the letter from Colonel Delamere. He was quiet for a little while, seated motionless in front of Eric's desk, gazing almost vacantly out of the window towards the Quayside. But his mind would be working furiously, Eric had no doubt, in spite of his calm exterior. As a professional civil servant, Eric surmised, he would be devious, inscrutable, with motives that would rarely appear on the surface.

'I understand that the statuette is no longer in the possession of . . . the estate,' Linwood-Forster remarked at last in a thoughtful tone.

'You've heard about the burglary. Yes, it seems the statuette was taken from Delamere Hall in the course of a robbery. Colonel Delamere was attacked during that burglary.'

'And has since died. A sad end for such a gallant, and loyal gentleman.' Almost casually, Linwood-Forster added, 'All in all, most unfortunate. And of course you now have no idea of the whereabouts of this statuette.'

'None. Other than that it's probably in the hands of the men who burgled the Hall and attacked the colonel. But what's the particular reason for the Foreign Office's interest in the Anubis figure? Why did the colonel think you people should have it? I imagine it's a valuable object, and of some antiquity, but that hardly seems a good reason for Delamere wanting it to go into the hands of the department, rather than along with his other bequests to the museum in Newcastle.'

Linwood-Forster put the tips of his fingers together, pressed them lightly to his mean lips. 'I don't think we need go into such matters for the time being. It is enough that you are aware that Her Majesty's Government is interested in the recovery of the statuette as quickly as possible.'

'The government? The Foreign Office, you mean. You were slow enough to act on the matter when the colonel was alive.'

Linwood-Forster's eyes clouded over. 'His original letter to us some time ago. Ah, yes, well that is another matter. But, as to the reasons why we should now want to secure the object, you ask the question . . . and it is possible your mind will continue to be exercised on the matter. Particularly if the statuette should by chance fall into your possession again.'

There was a short silence. Linwood-Forster gazed out of the window, watching the slow manoeuvring of a Norwegian frigate tying up at the Quayside. He cleared his throat. 'My long experience of human nature,' he said after a while, 'leads me to believe that it is better that answers be provided, in some cases before questions are even asked. There are occasions when probing can turn over stones that are best left undisturbed, and if the answers are freely given in the first instance, continued searching no longer becomes necessary.'

'Am I likely to be asking difficult questions at some time in the future?' Eric queried.

The thin smile had returned, containing no trace of humour. 'It is possible. And in the present . . . ah . . . delicate international situation it is perhaps better that you be . . . dissuaded from asking further questions.'

'Aren't you afraid I might use what information you give me for purposes you might regard as unwise?'

Linwood-Forster raised an elegant eyebrow. 'I think we have dealt with that danger, surely? There is the matter of client confidentiality: we are now, of course, one of your clients.

But even apart from that there are other ways of making sure you would not profit from such behaviour. The Law Society . . . a word dropped in the right place . . .'

'The full power of the Crown.' Eric smiled. 'Is such majesty really necessary, to threaten a small-time solicitor on Tyneside?'

'Threaten? By no means. But it is perhaps wiser that we in responsible office take no chances. And what I tell you will not be disclosed by you . . . In any case, if you were to bruit the information abroad, it would be derided, of course, denied and dismissed out of hand.'

'So why—'

'We would prefer that certain information did not come into the public domain. Particularly not at this time.' Linwood-Forster's eyes were lidded as he contemplated his slim fingers. 'The fact is, the Anubis statuette is an artefact of some ancient provenance. From what we understand, it was taken from the tomb of Tutankhamun, in 1922.'

He clearly expected Eric to be surprised. After a short silence Eric asked casually, 'You mean by Howard Carter!'

Linwood-Forster sniffed, suffering a small disappointment. 'Either he, or his patron Lord Carnarvon.'

'I was at Delamere Hall,' Eric said slowly, 'when I heard the story of the looting of the tomb. And you're now telling me that the Anubis figure was one of the items taken.'

'We believe that to be the case. It was taken by one man or the other,' Linwood-Forster conceded. 'We think thereafter it was placed for safe keeping in the hands of—'

'The Bethell family?' Eric hazarded.

Linwood-Forster's hands were very still. 'We think that is likely. So . . . you are aware of the suggested involvement of Lord Westbury and his son.'

'Colonel Delamere had an old friend. He talked of the Bethells. He's half-convinced they were murdered, all those years ago.'

Linwood-Forster affected to be shocked. 'Really? How fanciful. And this gentleman . . . ?'

'Neil Scanlon. A writer. A conspiracy theorist.'

Linwood-Forster's brow was furrowed momentarily, then cleared. 'Ah. Mr Scanlon. Yes . . . his name has come to our attention . . .'

Eric sat back in his chair, and waited.

At last, with a sigh, Linwood-Forster shifted, uncrossed his lean legs, smoothed again at his trousers. 'Ah, well, I think it would be best, in the circumstances, if I were to fill in a little of the background which so many people seem to find so intriguing. Certain irrefutable facts are at our fingertips. But while the facts are there, the relevant interpretations have not been made, the links not explored.' He paused, held Eric's glance for a moment. 'You are then aware, I imagine, that the wife of the fifth Lord Carnarvon was an illegitimate daughter of Alfred de Rothschild, founder of the British branch of the House of Rothschild, the wealthiest and most powerful Jewish family in Europe?'

Eric shook his head. 'I'm not familiar with her history. Only that she obtained the concession to continue excavation at the tomb of Tutankhamun, with Carter as her chief excavator.'

'Lady Almina . . . mixed French and Spanish extraction. And a woman of, shall we say, remarkable sexual appetite . . . But no need to go into that. For our purposes we need say no more than that when Alfred de Rothschild died, he left a large part of his fortune to Almina and her children. Nothing to Lord Carnarvon — who, after his expenditure in the Valley of Kings, was in straitened financial circumstances.'

'So I understand.'

'This is probably why, respected and experienced excavator as he was, along with Carter he decided to remove items from the tomb, to make up for what he had spent over the years . . . in case the Egyptian government refused to honour their commitments under the concession.'

'Which they did.'

'Indeed,' Linwood-Forster agreed drily. 'One of the items taken we believe to have been the Anubis figure. It was handed to the Bethells for safe keeping. Later, after their deaths, it seems to have disappeared.'

'You've no idea what happened to it?' Eric asked, surprised.

'Let's say we have *certain* information. The daughter of a cousin . . . a nephew who was a collector . . . a possible auction at Sotheby's. All so long ago. And things get forgotten . . . other urgent matters intrude . . . We have managed to trace — somewhat late in the day — the likely movements of the statuette. The final link to Colonel Delamere we were not aware of. But it seems that to the good colonel it came.'

'And he wanted it to go to the Foreign Office,' Eric mused. 'But why? Was he trying to make amends for an eighty-year-old theft?'

'Hard words, Mr Ward.' Linwood-Forster shrugged. 'We should not impute simply larcenous intentions to the parties concerned. But no, it was more than that. We believe that Colonel Delamere had come to appreciate the true value of the statuette.'

'Which was?'

Linwood-Forster lifted his narrow chin in disdain. 'Not just financial, I assure you. No . . . all I wish to say at the moment is that the Anubis statuette is linked to a curious incident that occurred in the spring of 1923. At the British Embassy a furious quarrel broke out between Howard Carter and a certain vice-consul. The roots of that quarrel . . . well, shall we say for the moment merely that it was linked to the Anubis statuette.' He hesitated, then making an abrupt decision, rose to his feet. 'But perhaps I have already said more than I should, Mr Ward. Suffice to add this. The Foreign Office failed to get hold of the statuette from Carter at that time. It was offered to us some months ago, but unfortunately . . . well, never mind about that. Suffice it to say that we would like to get hold of it now. As quickly as possible.' He fixed Eric with a stony glare. 'Before the damned thing falls into the wrong hands.'

As if startled by his own vehemence, he walked stiffly towards the door. At the doorway he paused, looked back.

'So, Mr Ward, if by any chance in the near future you should happen to discover the whereabouts of the statuette, you will keep quiet about it, won't you — and make arrangements for the last wishes of Colonel Delamere to be carried out.' He paused, eyed Eric sternly. 'Discreetly, of course.'

After he left, Eric felt he detected the faint hint of sub-terfuge in the air. It smelt sour, stale and pervasive.

CHAPTER 3

DCI Charlie Spate disliked mortuaries. It was not so much the sight of corpses, the waxy sheen of the skin, the stiff limbs, the various insanities that had been visited upon them by deranged psychopaths, jealous husbands, or zealous pathologists. After all, he had seen enough bodies dragged out of the Thames, and latterly the Tyne; he'd retrieved a headless suicidal corpse on a railway line; he'd fished around in a well for discarded body parts and he knew well the smell of burning human flesh. It wasn't any of that. It was just the odours of formaldehyde and the general attitude prevailing.

And it was the same with forensic laboratories.

He could have sent Elaine, or the liaison officer who maintained the links between the pathologists and the investigating officers. But he decided to go himself to Gosforth, simply because he didn't like going there. He could be that stubborn from time to time. And it would take his mind off that damned woman, who had coolly explained to him when he suggested he came around to her place that she didn't think it was a good idea that particular evening.

Next thing, she'd be telling him she was staying in to wash her hair.

The pathologist was a ruddy-faced Scotsman called Billy McLeod, who was built like a front-row forward. He had the neck of one, a badly rearranged nose, piggy little eyes and he shambled like a Neanderthal. He was hairy, too. Charlie had disliked him on sight. Though at the moment, he was disliking everyone.

'So, what you got, Doc?' he asked, making no attempt to cloak his sullenness.

The pathologist didn't seem to notice. He dropped heavily into a chair and yawned, scratched at his hairy neck. 'Been up all night. Bloody priorities! You people . . . why can't you find bodies during the day, instead of always at night?'

It wasn't Charlie's case he was referring to. He wasn't interested. 'You get anything from the Delamere stiff?'

The pathologist eyed him disdainfully. 'Oh, that one . . .' He frowned, pursed his lips. 'I did some work for you recently, didn't I? You'll forgive me, I'm new around here and not too good on names. You are—'

'DCI Spate.' Charlie almost spat out the words. He knew very well the pathologist recognised him. It was a game he was playing: he disliked Charlie just as Charlie couldn't stand him. In fact, Charlie didn't like any Scots, really.

'Ah, yes. DCI Spate . . . It was you and your henchmen who let that case blow up in our faces the other day.'

The comment was unreasonable, and inaccurate.

Charlie was about to remonstrate — it had, after all, been a mix-up at the lab as well — but then he decided it wasn't worth pursuing. 'Delamere,' he said stubbornly.

McLeod yawned again. He had sparkling white teeth. Maybe he scrubbed them in formaldehyde. 'You won't be asking about the cause of death, I imagine. Took quite a heavy blow to the head. That's what finished him off.' He eyed Charlie coldly. 'I'm using layman's language, of course, since you fellers get so easily confused.'

Charlie opened his mouth to make a sharp retort, but thought better of it. He simply scowled instead.

'Anyway,' the pathologist continued, 'we picked up nothing of significance from the body. The old man must have marched along that corridor, confronted one of the two men—'

'So you've established there *were* two men involved in the robbery.'

'Confronted one of the two men,' McLeod glared, irritated at the interruption, 'swinging his walking stick, and that's when the second of the men clobbered him from behind. Something heavy but not too heavy . . . interesting sort of weapon, really.'

'What are you talking about? Interesting?'

'Not your run-of-the-mill weapon,' the pathologist replied, rubbing one eye wearily. 'Not your usual axe, or club, or knife. No, this was quite different.'

'In what way?' Charlie prompted, as Billy McLeod showed signs of wanting to go to sleep.

'Difficult to say with any precision — and I know you guys like precision — but my guess is the weapon would have been made of some hard wood. But the funny thing is it was tipped with metal.'

'How do you mean?' Charlie asked, puzzled.

The pathologist blinked, opened his eyes wide, and grimaced. 'The weight of the blow — and it was a pretty hefty smack — drove the end of the club, or whatever it was, into the back of Delamere's skull. But the entry deep into the skull was achieved by something sharp, long, narrow, pointed. Almost chisel-like, if you want a picture.'

Charlie made no attempt to keep the disdain out of his voice. 'So it was a club with a sharp point. There's a whole range of things that could fit that description.'

'Not many would be tipped with gold,' McLeod replied calmly.

Charlie stared at him. Almost stupidly, he repeated, 'Gold?'

McLeod permitted himself a vague smile, having grabbed Charlie's attention at last. 'Yes, interesting isn't it?

A club of some sorts, metal tipped to a sharp point . . . but then we find traces of gold leaf in among the shards of bone in the skull.'

Both men fell silent. Charlie waited for a further explanation, but none was forthcoming. McLeod was going to make him sweat. Finally, Charlie gave in. 'OK, so what do you make of that?' Charlie demanded.

McLeod shook his head. 'Hey, I don't come to conclusions. That's your job, theories. I deal in facts. And I've just given them to you. But I'm a generous man. I stick my neck out occasionally, for *friends*. My guess is that this wasn't a weapon the robbers took along with them. I mean, you don't go armed with a gold-topped stick when you step into the dark night determined on villainous enterprises, do you?'

'What exactly are you trying to tell me?' Charlie asked suspiciously, wary of the ironic suggestion they were buddies.

'Since you can't deduce what I mean from the facts I'll help you,' McLeod replied, stretching his arms above his head and sighing. 'The weapon used by the killer was something he'd picked up at the scene of the crime.'

'Like what?'

'How should I know? But if I were you, I'd take a close look at the list of stuff that's said to be missing. Maybe you'll find a description there of an artefact that would fit the bill. Only a suggestion, of course.'

Charlie had received the inventory from Eric Ward that morning. He frowned. He'd run through the list in a perfunctory manner before coming out to the Gosforth labs, but maybe McLeod had a point. He'd have to take a closer look.'

His mobile phone rang. McLeod leant back in his chair and closed his eyes, duty done as far as he was concerned. Charlie switched on the phone.

'Charlie?' It was Elaine.

'I'm at the labs,' he growled, still out of sorts with her because of her rejection.

'Better get your arse back here. Conference in half an hour.'

'Conference?'

'Three-line whip. It's Charteris again. And he didn't sound best pleased.'

'Is the bastard ever?' Charlie grumbled.

He snapped shut the phone. McLeod opened his eyes. 'Bad news?' he smiled, hopefully.

Charlie grunted. 'I got to get back to headquarters. Is that all you got for me so far?'

'With regard to the body, yes. There was no physical contact between the killer and Delamere, none at least that we were able to pick up on — no flakes of skin, hair, anything like that — so that part of the search has been unproductive.'

He was holding something back. 'What else?' Charlie snapped, impatient.

'Well, as I say, nothing on the body. But in the office itself . . .'

'Tell me,' Charlie snarled, wanting to get away.

'They used something to smash the front of the glass display case. One of the intruders reached in, grabbed stuff from the case. In doing so he scratched himself. We managed to pick up a blood sample. And, due to the wonders of modern science, DCI Spate, we were able to make a match.'

'You got a DNA match?' Charlie wondered.

'Just that,' McLeod replied smugly. 'A match with someone we already had on our books, in a manner of speaking.'

'So you can identify exactly who broke into that place . . . You got a name for me?'

McLeod nodded, his eyes sparkling maliciously as he regarded Charlie. 'I got a name for you. I just hope you don't go buggering this one up.'

And when he told Charlie the name, Charlie was so pleased he could have kissed him. In spite of the hairiness.

As he drove back to headquarters in Ponteland, jubilation coursed through his veins. For more reasons than one.

* * *

He was late attending the conference in the room set aside by Assistant Chief Constable Charteris. Charlie mumbled an apology and sat down; Charteris glared at him and curled a contemptuous lip. It was clear he had not recovered his temper: he was suffering under a long-running resentment. Perhaps it had something to do with the two strangers who flanked him.

One was a thickset man with fair hair, cut short. He sat squarely in his chair behind the table, arms folded so that all could see the bulge of honed muscle under his jacket. His eyebrows were knitted in a frown that Charlie guessed would be habitual; his eyes were slate-grey and unforgiving; his jaw seemed to jut defiance and contempt, as though he owed nothing, denied everything, and would always go his own way without remorse. He had a stiff back. He was his own man. Charlie rather approved of him: if he was in a tight corner, this character would be the one to have beside him. Or at his back. As for the other man, in the pin-striped suit, Charlie dismissed him immediately: a typical civil servant, all flannel, precision and deceit.

'Now that DCI Spate has deigned to join us, maybe we can get on,' Charteris said balefully. Charlie glanced around the room: Elaine was there, so was Sam Macmillan, and a few other men he knew vaguely, from the South Tyneside group. So it was another bloody joint operation.

'You've been brought together,' Charteris continued in a harsh, unwilling tone, 'to bring you up to date on developments with regard to your activities on the investigation into the fire-bombing incidents at the shipping agency in Jarrow. Prior to this, as I understand from some of the comments that have been made, you have been somewhat concerned at the direction which has been taken on these matters. You will also be aware that the young delinquents who undertook the fire-bombing have been identified, but for the time being it has been decided that no action be taken against them. They will, of course, be kept under surveillance.' He paused, took cognisance of the dissatisfied murmur that arose in the room, then took a deep breath. 'I will leave it to Major Cryer to explain.'

Major? Charlie shifted in his seat and glanced at Elaine. She failed to meet his eye: stiff-backed, arms folded across her breasts, she was watching as the thickset man with the hard face rose from his seat. He stepped back, turned to look briefly at the screen that had been erected behind him. He nodded to someone at the back of the room. Lights were dimmed. Charlie started, looked about him. This was going to be a bloody film show!

A projector flashed on behind him. A picture of a man's head appeared on the screen behind Major Cryer. It was a head and shoulders shot: the man had a lean face and dark piercing eyes, heavily lidded, a prominent beak of a nose. His hair was black, curly, straggling down over his forehead. He wore a heavy beard which hid his mouth and chin. There was nothing pleasant about his appearance: he wore a heavy scowl.

'His name is Ismail Badur,' Major Cryer announced. 'It's believed he is Pakistani in origin, but we've not been able to verify that. Certainly, he spent some time in Afghanistan, slipping back across the Pakistan border from time to time, and we have evidence that he has attended training schools set up by al-Qaeda — schools specialising in terrorist techniques. He's thirty-two years old, is suspected of having been involved in activities against American Embassies in Egypt and Burma, and travels under various aliases. We know with certainty that he came in on a freighter from Abidjan some two months ago: he disembarked as a deck-hand, and made contact with certain other men of his persuasion in South Shields. He's a dangerous, committed man. He's here in the north-east, and our priority is to find him.'

'I'd settle for grabbing the two teenagers,' someone to Charlie's left muttered. Charteris picked it up, and scowled.

'I draw your attention to Ismail Badur,' Cryer went on, ignoring the interruption, 'because we believe he's planning something important here in the north-east. He's been brought in to head an existing organisation, albeit a small one — to which your teenagers were attracted, but are not really part of — which has as its purpose an event here on Tyneside. We're not certain what it might be—'

'Blowing up the Tyne Tunnel?' the earlier heckler queried. 'At least that would put an end to the bloody rush-hour queues.'

He was from south of the river. Charlie realised that the frustrations he'd been feeling were reciprocated on the other bank of the Tyne.

Cryer was unfazed. He shrugged diffidently. 'It could be something like that. Or the Tyne Bridge. Or the Metro system. But we don't think it's any of those things. All we do know is that there's been a great deal of electronic chatter going on, and we're convinced something is about to happen up here — which we need to stop.'

'Even if we don't know what it is?' Charlie intervened himself. He was not about to be shown backward, in front of the South Tyneside mob, who were showing signs of unrest at the suggestion there was a terrorist cell working on their patch. 'Is this why we've been stumbling around with hands and feet tied recently? Why no one seems to be able to tell us what the hell is going on? And just what are *you* all about, Major Cryer. What's your part in all this?' *Sotto voce,* he added, 'Why, *Major,* for God's sake?'

The lowering of his voice hadn't been enough. For a moment Charlie thought that Charteris, in spite of his own frustrations, was going to explode. Instead, as he struggled to his feet, glaring at Charlie, he was forestalled by the pin-striped civil servant, who raised a hand, smiled thinly at the assistant chief constable, and suggested, 'Perhaps I should have a word. To sketch in the background in this matter.' He glanced over his shoulder at the image of the man Major Cryer had identified as a terrorist and then leant forward, to face the assembled police officers. 'My name is Linwood-Forster. I hold a position — for my sins — in the Foreign

Office. And in order that you should not doubt the credentials of Major Cryer I will explain to you that he is a much trusted field officer. While normally he works in Army Intelligence — and has recently returned from Iraq — he is presently seconded to MI6.' He bestowed a benign smile on the hunched, heavy-shouldered figure beside him. 'We have every confidence in him. But I seem to detect a certain reluctance in the audience to contemplate the existence of a terrorist cell here in the north-east. Forgive me if I give you certain background facts which may not be known to you.'

He cleared his throat delicately. Charlie thought he looked like a university lecturer about to launch on a favourite theme. His voice was thin; his diction precise. 'It may surprise some of you to know that there has been a long history of Arab involvement at South Shields. It would surprise for instance you, Mr Spate.'

Charlie started. How the hell did this bloody civil servant know him by name? He glanced at Charteris. Briefing. It would be all about briefing.

'For instance,' Linwood-Forster continued, 'perhaps you are not aware that as long ago as Roman times a naval squadron was sent from the Tigris in Iraq to patrol the river mouth of the Tyne. It was an important trading centre. So important, the Romans built a fort on the Lawe headland on the south bank of the river: the fort was called *Arbei.'* He gave a condescending smile. 'For those among you who are not classicists, that means the *Place of the Arabs.'*

'That's as may be,' Charlie growled, resenting that he had been picked out, that they were being spoken down to, and resenting what was beginning to sound like a history lesson. 'But it's a far cry from suggesting there's a nest of terrorists located in the town. Two thousand years is a long time ago . . .'

'Oh, there's much more recent activity from the Middle East,' Linwood-Forster demurred smoothly. 'During the First World War, with so many men called away to fight in the trenches of France and Belgium, there was a considerable

96

shortage of manpower in the shipyards. So Swan Hunter and other shipbuilding companies drafted in a labour force from the Middle East. You can imagine the consequences.'

'Such as?' Charlie challenged.

'Race riots.' Linwood-Forster's lips creased in a thin, ironic smile. 'As late as 1930, I believe the *South Shields Gazette* was reporting racist attacks in the town. The reality was, of course, that the motivation was largely economic. The war-shattered men who had been promised a new life came back to find their jobs had been taken by dark-skinned strangers who had settled in the town.'

'Even so—'

'And apart from the men who settled in South Shields, and raised families there — among whom there are many disaffected, unemployed young men — you need to be aware of the considerable river traffic that still makes its way into the Tyne from overseas. Freighters come in from Limassol and Panama, Valetta and Nassau, Monrovia, Sevastopol and Riga. Among the sailors there are some, no doubt, whose papers are perhaps somewhat manufactured. Like our friend, Ismail Badur.'

Charlie Spate leant back in his chair and frowned at the assistant chief constable. He was tempted to ask what the hell this had to do with his being taken off the South Tyne enquiry — which was what this conference seemed to be all about — to concentrate on the break-in at Delamere Hall. Charteris was glaring at him, all ready to tear at him given the chance. Charlie thought discretion the wiser course.

Linwood-Forster still held the floor. 'Major Cryer has already commented upon the fact that we have recently become aware of a considerable increase in the amount of electronic chatter relating to a certain event — which we need not refer to at this moment — and this is why it was thought best to bring in Major Cryer. The Major is an expert in intelligence—'

'Counter-intelligence,' Cryer interrupted. He hunched his shoulders, leaning forward, well able to speak for and defend himself. 'Counter-Intelligence, and the rank is unimportant.' He fixed Charlie with a cold, penetrative glance. 'You, I believe, are DCI Spate.'

Everyone around the room seemed to know who he was, and he was being picked on. Charlie resented it. 'That's right. And I was working south of the Tyne. Now I've been dragged off the enquiry — which I gather you're involved in — and pushed off onto a burglary in Northumberland. Which has now turned into a murder enquiry.' He took a deep breath, and glared at Assistant Chief Constable Charteris. 'Not that I'm owed any explanation, it seems, for this way of going on.'

He felt: Elaine's eyes upon him. He darted a glance sideways: he read sympathy in her face. Maybe tonight he'd be in with a chance. It had been some weeks since . . .

Major Cryer broke into his mental wandering as Charteris sat there fuming, perhaps at his own impotence. 'Your stepping away from targeting the South Shields terrorist cell—'

'I didn't even know there was one!' Charlie burst out.

'—your stepping away, the decision to pull you off to deal with the burglary at Delamere Hall, it was a snap decision, DCI Spate, made for operational reasons, on my recommendation and after discussion with your Chief Constable.' He slipped a glance at Charteris, thunder-browed at his side. 'At that time, we felt it best to keep everything under wraps. But now, since Colonel Delamere has died, and certain artefacts are missing, we think it is perhaps best that we put you in the picture. Your enquiries into the Delamere burglary are high priority, I assure you.'

There was a short silence. Charlie folded his arms, gritted his teeth. What the hell was going on here? Typical of civil servants and spooks, making everything a bloody sight more complicated than it should be. This garbage they were dishing up . . . what was the point of it when he had the answers they needed already? And since when did police operations come under the orders and direction of MI6 and the bloody Foreign Office?

Linwood-Forster was taking the floor again. 'The group as a whole can now be informed that each of you have one thing to concentrate upon. One thing. One person. *Ismail Badur.* We need to find him. Quickly. But he is a dangerous man, and we will now be talking to both Chief Constables about the need for some of you to be given licences to carry arms. We have the names of certain members of the terrorist cell, and they will be under constant surveillance, but it is Ismail Badur whom we wish this group to concentrate on. And find. South of the river, undercover officers will continue surveillance on members of the cell. Even the fringe teenagers. The members, and their families — innocent though relations may be — will also be monitored. And as for you, DCI Spate, we have no wish to interfere with your investigations. We merely wish that you would expedite the enquiry, find out what was taken from Delamere Hall, recover it, and at the same time — as they say in American films — bring us the head of Ismail Badur!'

Linwood-Forster was clearly pleased at what he regarded as a topical reference, a demonstration that he could come down to their level with ease. Charlie slowly unfolded his arms. These smooth bastards had told them little, if anything. 'Am I supposed to gather from this that you believe your terrorist group was involved at Delamere Hall?'

The room was silent for several seconds. Major Cryer glanced at Linwood-Forster, who nodded a brief assent. Cryer turned back to look at Charlie. 'We have every reason to believe so, yes.'

'That's hard to accept,' Charlie asserted confidently, 'in view of the evidence. I think you're barking up the wrong tree.'

Cryer's mouth hardened. 'That may be your view, DCI Spate, but it's not ours. The fact is, it's become clear to us over the last few months that something of significance is happening here on Tyneside, and specifically in South Shields. We've been aware for a considerable time that there's a loosely knit cell operating in this area, in touch with agents in Pakistan and Afghanistan. We have been of the opinion that they posed no immediate danger, that they were largely amateurish, in spite of the training that several of them had received in camps linked to al-Qaeda operations. But recently things have changed somewhat.'

'They've started building a bomb or something?' Charlie scoffed. 'If that's so you should have pulled in the bastards!' He was encouraged by a low murmur of approval from the room.

'It's not quite that simple,' Cryer replied coldly. 'As you are no doubt aware. The fact is the electronic chatter emanating from this part of the world suddenly seems to have increased in amount and urgency. We are not yet certain what it's all about, what is planned, quite who is involved. But some things have become clear. In some way or another, Colonel Delamere was involved.'

'Delamere?' Charlie shook his head in puzzlement. 'You saying he was involved in terrorism activity?'

'The nature of his involvement,' Linwood-Forster intervened gravely, 'is not yet entirely clear to us, and what we do know I'm afraid must remain within our possession for the time being.'

Charlie felt the triumph of certainty in his veins. 'So let's hear it again . . . you're saying that the burglars were Islamic terrorists? And you reckon it was this character—' he pointed to the screen behind Cryer, 'it was this Ismail Badur who broke into the Hall and clobbered the old man?'

Cryer was glaring at him, competitively. He gave a slow, deliberate nod. 'That's it. Exactly.'

Charlie could have exploded the whole thing right there and then. But he was eaten up with pent-up rage at these men who thought they knew it all. They had pulled Home Office, Foreign Office and MI6 rank on the Chief Constable, leant on him to keep Charteris largely in the dark, he could see that now, and had them all running around like headless chickens, with no sense of direction. All the while they'd been playing their own cloak-and-dagger games: they were terrorist-hunting freaks, who were unable to see what was there right in front of their noses.

He grunted to himself in satisfaction. Well, let them stew in their own prejudices, poke into any dark corners they wanted. DCI Charlie Spate was not about to enlighten them. They'd given him licence to get on with the break-in at Delamere Hall, and the killing of the colonel. A warm, exulting glow began to rise in his chest. Let them get on with their own party games, scurrying along the track of their false, wild goose chase.

Because he already knew who had broken into Delamere Hall. He knew who had clobbered the old man. And it was Charlie Spate who was going to nail the bastard. Not Cryer. Not Linwood-Forster. Charlie Spate. He glanced triumphantly across the room at Elaine Start. He could already imagine the enthusiasm she'd show when he got back into her bed, triumphant.

He was about to go across to speak to her as the meeting broke up, but was frustrated when Linwood-Forster, with Major Cryer at his side, stepped down towards him, raising a hand. Scowling, Charlie waited.

'DCI Spate. A word, if you please.'

It was Major Cryer who spoke, however. 'I gain the impression you don't agree with our methods, Mr Spate. But this business really is of the utmost importance.'

'Why?' Charlie rasped, irritated by the man's composure.

Cryer regarded him blandly for several seconds. His left hand strayed towards his mouth, stroked his lower lip thoughtfully. He was controlling his feelings, choosing his words with care. 'Mr Linwood-Forster has explained to the group some of the background. Perhaps it is appropriate that I add a little more — in strict confidence, of course, so as not to endanger current operations—'

'You're suggesting I could bugger things up? Current operations? Here in our manor?'

'You are somewhat possessive in your attitudes, Mr Spate,' Linwood-Forster observed coldly. 'We should be clear about this: you may see this as a purely local affair, but I assure you we are talking here of national interests, rather than local preoccupations.'

'I'm still struggling to find out just what is going on,' Charlie snapped. 'But don't worry. I won't botch up any of your little games. I'll just get on with the stuff on my own plate.'

Major Cryer stepped closer. There was no emotion in his tone, or in his eyes. 'That's fine, but we need to be clear about this, Mr Spate. The two operations — the hunt for Ismail Badur, and your own investigation at Delamere Hall — are closely linked. So, don't get too independent, Mr Spate. Keep us informed.'

In a pig's eye, Charlie thought, as he nodded and turned away to follow Elaine Start from the room.

* * *

When the rest of the material arrived from Bradley and Tindall Eric knew he would have enough work on his hands for the rest of the year. Whatever the true motives behind Linwood-Forster's decision, it was clear that through his new clients Eric stood to make a better income than he had achieved for some years — not since he had been married to Anne, in fact, and working on her behalf.

Not that he was strongly motivated by money. As long as he made enough to keep his head above water he was happy enough — that, and the fact that the kind of work he undertook gave him a degree of satisfaction — in spite of the occasional guilt over people like his recent client Joe Fisher. The briefs he was now preparing for Sharon Owen were absorbing, however: they were mainly immigration issues, applications from Poles and Romanians and Somalis to obtain residence in Britain, a few appeals against decisions already made, and queries regarding work permits, student visas and other similar problems arising from the wave of new entrants arriving as a result of the accession of new countries to the European Union. Everyone seemed to be wanting to come to the UK to obtain economic benefits . . . and there was very little that was being done as yet to stop them. He was still slightly puzzled at Linwood-Forster's dismissive answer to his query that these matters were normally handled by the Home Office. But it was work, and it was lucrative, so he shrugged mentally and battled on.

Eric was working at his desk when his secretary rang through from the outer office. 'I forgot to mention, Mr Ward. There was a woman rang through earlier; you weren't available at the time, but she said she'd ring back.'

'She give a name?' Eric queried.

'Miss Castle.'

Eric hesitated. It had been three weeks now since he had met Sarah Castle at Delamere Hall; she had agreed they might meet again, but had insisted she would contact him. Till now, she hadn't done so. He'd more or less given up on her, though he still thought a little about her occasionally. Now that she'd made contact at last, as she'd promised, he felt a stir of interest again.

'If she calls again, Susie, put her straight through.'

He was somewhat concerned about his secretary. Normally, she was quick, efficient and smart: she often guessed what he needed even before he knew it himself. But of late she had seemed preoccupied, and her work had become erratic. He'd considered taking her on one side and having a chat, finding out if she needed a break from work, or whether something was bothering her that he could help with. But he'd been busy, preoccupied, there had been the funeral of Colonel Delamere to attend to, he'd spent some time with Anne going over the contracts that she had negotiated with Peter Felshaw, and then there were days when Susie seemed brighter, more like her old self . . . so he had put the matter to one side. But the call from Sarah Castle was another example. Susie had become forgetful, almost slapdash. It wasn't like her usual self. He would have to make time to talk to her.

It was almost an hour later that Susie rang through again. There was a shade of disapproval in her voice. 'Miss Castle said she'd call again, but she's actually arrived, Mr Ward. She's here in the office.'

Surprised, Eric stood up and walked across the room, opened the door, looked out into the anteroom used by his secretary. Sarah Castle was standing in front of Susie's desk. She smiled at him.

'Sarah! A surprise. Come on in.'

Susie studiously avoided looking at him as Sarah walked past Eric into his office. He closed the door quietly, turned to look at her.

'The elusive Sarah Castle. So you finally made it.'

Her laugh was light. 'Eric, I'm sorry, I did say I'd get in contact with you again, but things have been a bit hectic. I've been down to London for a while, and then I had to go to Leeds.'

'Still on your assignment?'

She nodded. 'That's right. Felshaw's firm have offices all over the place, it seems, and there've been various people I needed to meet.'

'What exactly is this journalistic assignment you're working on?' Eric asked curiously, waving her to take a chair. He hesitated, then returned to his own chair behind the desk. She sat down. She was wearing a light top, and short skirt. She crossed her legs in a casual, fluid motion. Her legs were long, bare, slim. She seemed very much at ease as she glanced around at his office.

'Very boring, I assure you. Nothing that you'd find interesting. Sort of history of the firm, and putting together a presentational package . . . my God, it bores even me to talk about it. Anyway, how are you?'

'Pleased to see you again.'

She chuckled. 'Well, I know I've been remiss. But I meant what I said: I was hoping we'd get together again soon.'

'How soon?'

She cocked her head to one side. 'How about lunch today?'

'That would suit me very well,' Eric agreed, casting a reluctant eye on the pile of papers on his desk. Susie would not be pleased by this decision.

Perhaps his reluctance was communicated to her. She smiled. 'If you're certain—'

'I'm certain,' he replied firmly.

'It'll be on me,' Sarah asserted.

'I—'

'No argument. Just had my monthly retainer come in so I'm flush. And this way, it gets to be my choice of restaurant.'

'You have a place in mind?'

There was a slight hesitation, as though she was casting around for an answer. 'I've heard of a good Greek restaurant in the Bigg Market. I thought we could maybe try a bottle of their Retsina. How would that suit you?'

It suited Eric fine.

She hesitated, glanced about her again, as though a little uncertain, and then she asked, 'One small problem, though. Would you mind if I made a phone call? I wasn't sure whether you'd be able to make it for lunch, not at such short notice, and I had a business meeting scheduled this afternoon—'

'If that's a problem—' Eric began.

'No, no, it's not a problem, but if I could just make a brief call—'

'Be my guest,' Eric replied, waving to the phone. 'I'll just go have a word with Susie.'

He left the room, closing the door behind him so that Sarah could have privacy for her phone call. Susie looked up. 'I'll be out for lunch,' he explained. 'I don't believe I have any pressing appointments directly after lunch?'

Susie's lips were set primly, and disapproval registered in her tone, a flash of the old Susie he had been missing of late. 'You'd set aside the afternoon for the files, Mr Ward.'

Eric smiled. 'I'll be back to slave away, don't worry about it, Susie. But I'd better have a look at the appointments book for the next couple of days . . . I've lost touch a bit, with all the stuff you've piled on my desk . . .'

Sarah Castle's call seemed to be taking longer than she had anticipated. Eric waited in the outer office, making a show of scanning the appointments book, under Susie's stern eye. At last the door opened, and his guest emerged. 'All fixed,' she announced cheerfully.

'Are you ready to go?' he asked.

'Whenever you are.' She smiled at Susie. 'Nice to meet you.'

Eric wasn't sure that the feeling was reciprocated. But then, Susie had always liked Anne.

As they left the office together, Eric was aware of a certain tightness in his chest. They had not spent a great deal of time together, he and Sarah Castle, but as they went out to his car he realised he was looking forward to the unexpected lunch appointment with considerable anticipation.

Like a schoolboy on a first date.

Although it was only a short distance to the restaurant the sky was grey, there was a hint of rain in the air so Eric decided to take the car. Sarah had come to his office by taxi, she explained. Eric managed to find a space to park his Celica in Grey Street. From there it was only a short walk to the restaurant Sarah had described, and she led the way down the steps to be greeted by the waitress, and led to a table. When she sat down he watched her: her eyes were sparkling; her lips full and red, her skin olive and smooth. He thought she looked very attractive, and told her so.

'I was told Englishmen were rarely charming,' she observed.

'They react when they have good reason to,' he explained.

They did not bother with an aperitif but went straight to the Retsina. It was not a wine Eric was very familiar with, but he enjoyed the pine resin flavour. Sarah ordered for them both, at his suggestion: he watched her while she pored over the menu, discussed it with the waiter — whose accent suggested to Eric that he had been raised far from Greece — and they began the meal with *dolmades*.

'So,' Sarah asked, 'What have you been up to?'

'Very busy,' Eric replied, and explained about the Foreign Office briefs. Her eyes widened and she raised an eyebrow.

'So I'm lucky to find you have time to relax!'

'It's not as bad as that,' Eric laughed.

She frowned slightly. 'I heard about the unfortunate death of Colonel Delamere. I would have liked to attend the funeral, even though I met him only once. You didn't know him well though, did you?'

Eric shook his head. 'No, but that day up at the Hall, after you'd left with Felshaw, I had a conference with Delamere. He asked me to act as executor to his will. Then, a week or so later, he was dead.'

She shook her head sadly. 'It was all so sudden . . . and he was such a nice, old-worldly gentleman. His executor, hey? Does his estate raise any great problems?'

'There are a few complications,' Eric murmured.

He hesitated, uncertain whether to tell her about the involvement of the Foreign Office, but decided against it. He had a duty of trust . . . and discretion. 'It'll all get sorted in due course.'

'And then there was the break-in that led up to his death,' she sighed. 'Did the burglars cause much damage?'

As she spoke she seemed a little restless, her eyes darting glances around the room. There was something almost mechanical in her conversation, and he got the impression her mind was elsewhere, as though she was only half-paying attention to what he was saying.

'They smashed some display cases, in an attempt to get their hands on the colonel's collection.'

'Did they get away with much?' she asked, her green eyes turning back to Eric.

'From what I've seen, checking the inventory, they didn't make off with a great deal.'

'Bad business, altogether.' She finished her *dolmades,* leant back in her seat, and regarded him thoughtfully. 'Of course, since Colonel Delamere died of his injuries, I imagine the police will now be deeply involved. What would have been just a case of burglary, it's now turned into a case of murder.'

Eric nodded. 'That's right. The first day I went up to the Hall the police were crawling all over the place.'

'Well, let's hope they get the people concerned, and soon,' she said. 'Now, you must tell me what you make of the fish . . .'

For the next half-hour they chatted easily, about inconsequential matters. Several times Eric caught her observing him, as though she was trying to make up her mind about something; he felt also there was a certain flirtatious manner in which she held his glance. He became very aware of her perfume, the line of her throat, and the way her body moved under the light top she wore.

He found himself talking about personal matters, about Anne and the break-up of their marriage, about his life in the police force before he had become a solicitor. She seemed disinclined to talk much about herself. He had been careful with the wine, drinking slowly because he had work to do that afternoon, but Sarah seemed happy to finish the bottle. At last, she glanced at her watch and shook her head. 'Hey, I've got to shift myself. I think I'd better attend the meeting after all. Eric, do you think you could give me a lift across the river?'

'Not a problem.'

She called the waiter, paid the bill in spite of Eric's protest, cast one last searching glance around the room and led the way up the stairs to the street outside. It had begun to rain. They ran down the side street, Eric holding her hand, until they reached the car. He unlocked the door, she slid inside, laughing, while he hurried to the driver's door.

They crossed the Tyne Bridge and headed for Jarrow.

As they drove, she searched in her handbag. 'Damned keys . . .' With a sudden surge of impatience she turned the contents of her handbag into her lap, spreading her legs wide, and Eric caught a glimpse of her slim thighs. Then she muttered a curse in a language he did not understand, as the keys she sought fell to the floor of the car. She leant sideways, but had some difficulty retrieving them, as she groped around underneath the seat.

'I'm afraid this model isn't very conducive to wriggling around in,' Eric apologised.

'I'll remember to keep that in mind,' she replied, looking at him archly, one eyebrow raised. 'I've got the damned things now. Keys to the office Felshaw's assigned to me.' She straightened up, put things away again in her handbag.

A few minutes later, they were pulling up, at her direction, in front of the office block that housed the shipping agency. 'So this is where you spend your time,' Eric commented.

'Less and less of it, seems to me. Anyway, I'd better run.' She hesitated, fixed him with her glance, and said, 'I really enjoyed lunch.'

'So did I.'

'To be honest, I enjoyed it more than I expected.' She put her hand on his arm and then, unexpectedly, leant over and kissed him on the mouth. It was a light touch for a moment, and then it seemed to become more serious. He felt the light flick of her tongue, and he responded; the grip on his arm tightened, and suddenly she shifted in the seat, her thigh pressing against his. They remained like that for several seconds, then she pulled back. Her eyes were wide and bright.

'I'd been wondering what that would be like.'

'Just curiosity?'

She smiled. 'Something more than that. I . . . look, I've got to run now but maybe we could meet up again soon?'

'I think that's a good idea.'

'Friday evening?' Her hand was still on his arm. 'I think I'd prefer dinner to lunch. We'd have more time ahead of us . . . no pressure of business.'

'Friday is fine with me.'

'Same place?'

'Why not?'

She touched his cheek lightly with her fingers, left the car, and hurried into the building. He watched her go. He was still aware of the touch of her mouth on his. She was a very direct woman, but he had no problem with that. He guessed she would head very quickly for what she wanted. Whatever that might be. He reversed the car away from the kerb headed back down the cul-de-sac to the main road.

Susie would be fussing in the office, conscious of the files on his desk, wondering where the hell he was. He rarely took a long lunch away from the office — unless it was a business meeting with a client. And she knew he'd been with Sarah Castle. He doubted that she'd be bearing an approving look, with so much work to be done.

When he entered the office, expecting reproof, he was surprised to see her keep her head down, almost ignoring him as she continued to work at the computer on the desk.

'Everything all right, Susie?' he asked, unable to keep the guilt out of his tone.

She merely nodded, didn't look up at him. Eric grimaced, and went into his office, sighed at the sight of the files, and slid behind his desk. This lot would keep him going until at least seven in the evening . . .

As he worked, his thoughts drifted from time to time to Sarah Castle. She interested him: she was bright, attractive and intelligent. But there was something else about her that he was unable to put his finger on: from time to time she wore a distracted air, her conversation seemed to move into automatic mode, as though she had something on her mind other than carrying on a social relationship. Maybe it was her work; perhaps she would be more relaxed when she met him again.

Dinner, on Friday, at the Greek restaurant . . .

Just before four o'clock Susie tapped on the door, and brought him a cup of coffee. He was immersed in the files, and merely nodded. She turned away, started to leave and then hesitated. He looked up after a moment, saw her standing in the doorway, staring at him. Her eyes were shadowed; she looked tired.

'You all right, Susie?'

She was silent for a few seconds, staring at him uncertainly, as though she wanted to say something, but was reluctant to begin. He tried to help her. He threw down his pen, leant back in his chair.

'Look, Susie, I've noticed you've not been yourself just recently,' he began. 'Is everything all right at home? You've been sort of distracted . . .'

She took a deep breath and shook her head. There was a certain sadness about her. He wondered if it was something to do with Sarah Castle, and then dismissed the thought as foolish.

After some hesitation, she said, 'Mr Ward, we've been together a long time.'

'We have that, indeed,' Eric replied gravely.

'I know there've been occasions when I almost . . . bully you, but you've taken it in good part—'

'It's what good secretaries do. I know you were merely trying to save me from myself,' he replied, smiling, trying to bring her out of her anxieties, whatever they might be.

'And I've always been loyal.'

'And outspoken,' he added.

'And straight,' she agreed.

Eric waited. 'So?'

She struggled to find the words. 'I'm afraid that's not been the case, just recently.'

Eric leant forward, forearms on the desk, puzzled. 'What's bothering you, Susie?'

'It's like I told you. I've not been straight with you.'

'What's this all about?' he asked, suddenly impatient at her reluctance to come out with what was bothering her.

She took a deep breath. 'I have an older sister.'

He knew very little about her family circumstances, other than that she was a widow, he understood. He supposed now he should have been more caring as an employer, found out more about her, but she had never been particularly forthcoming about her family background, and he had not pushed her. 'Does she live locally?' he asked carefully.

'Across the river. Down at Felling.'

He waited. She still seemed tongue-tied. And then suddenly it came out in a flood of words.

'There were three of us brought up in Felling. My father was a bricklayer, and he came from a bad family. Layabouts, mostly. But he was good to us as far as he was able: I mean, there was regular money coming in and he didn't knock my mam about at all. Things could have been worse. But my sister Jennie — she was his favourite. She couldn't do anything wrong in his eyes, and my brother Bill, well, his nose was out of joint, I think now, looking back. Anyway, he went off to the Navy. Drowned in the Persian Gulf they said. I hardly knew him, really, because I was so much younger than the others. Still, the loss of Bill hit my dad hard, and then, well . . . Jennie went off the rails.'

Susie stared at Eric, unwilling to go on but at the same time determined. Eric wondered where the story was leading.

'She got into drugs, ran around with bad company, and it broke my dad's heart. About ten years ago he fell off some scaffolding and was killed, but he hadn't seen Jennie for years before that. As for me, well I went my own way, ended up in a secretarial college, got married . . . not that that lasted long,' she said ruefully. 'He found someone prettier.'

'I thought you were widowed, Susie,' Eric said in surprise.

She shrugged. 'I hinted that was the way of it. Pride, I suppose. No, he left me.'

'He was a fool,' Eric commented quietly.

She managed a smile, but it had a weary edge. 'Then I came to work for you, Mr Ward, and things have been good. I've liked it here . . .'

'Tell me the problem,' Eric interrupted her quietly. 'It's to do with your sister?'

She hesitated, then nodded slowly. 'She had a child about seventeen years ago. Single mother, no income to speak of, I've helped her out from time to time, but . . . the thing is, Mr Ward, I've not been straight with you.'

'I don't understand.'

She raised her chin, met his glance almost defiantly. 'I should have told you before. But . . . it was pride, and I didn't think it would matter too much . . . the fact is, the young man you got off recently, that scallywag Joe Fisher . . . well, he's my nephew.'

'Your nephew?' Eric echoed in surprise.

Susie gritted her teeth. 'I've never liked him. Always arrogant, cocky, thought he knew it all. Never saw much of him really. But Jennie, she's never been able to control him, he needed a father's hand, she reckoned. And there wasn't one around. Joe's been in and out of trouble since he was twelve. We haven't had much to do with each other over the years, but then she came to me for help, over this latest business. She wanted assistance, advice . . . I suggested she get you to take up young Joe's defence. I . . .' She shifted uneasily. 'I said I'd pay the necessary fees.'

'Your nephew! Come on, Susie, you know paying me isn't necessary, and I'm sure Sharon Owen won't be pressing when she knows the circumstances.'

Susie's glance was stubborn. 'That's not the way it's got to be, Mr Ward. I owe you, and it'll be paid, but that's neither here nor there. Thing is, I should have told you at the time, been straight with you . . .'

She had been out of sorts for weeks, Eric realised.

Because she'd been afraid to tell him he was acting for her nephew, miserable at the thought she was keeping it from him, her pride gnawing at her, making it impossible for her to admit the relationship.

'Susie,' he began soothingly. 'You're making an issue out of nothing. There's no problem, believe me—'

A door slammed in the outer office. Susie started. 'Someone's come in,' she blurted out. 'Mr Ward, it's just I needed to say I was sorry, but that's not the end of it, because Jennie tells me—'

They heard a man's voice in the outer office, calling out. It carried a familiar, aggressive tone. Eric recognised the voice.

Susie began to open the door, turning away from Eric. As she did so, it was thrust open. A hard knot of anger formed in Eric's chest. The man was someone he recognised, and disliked. Detective Chief Inspector Charlie Spate.

'Not interrupting anything, am I?' Charlie Spate sneered. 'High-level consultations?'

Susie Cartwright shared Eric's feelings about Spate. His arrival seemed to bring the steel back into her. 'Perhaps we could talk later, Mr Ward,' she said. 'Assuming you have time for Mr Spate.'

'Oh, he'll have time,' Spate insisted breezily. 'This isn't going to take me long.' He stepped aside, gallantly waving his hand as Susie marched past him, head up. He eyed her ruefully. '*Some* women love me,' he called after her. She made no reply. He closed the door behind her, stood looking at Eric, a glint of pleasure in his eyes.

'You can spare me a few minutes, Mr Ward.'

'I'm busy,' Eric growled, pointing to the files on his desk. 'As you can see.'

'Well, I just thought it was time I brought you up to date with the Delamere business,' Charlie Spate announced airily and seated himself, very much at ease. 'Got the preliminary report in from forensics now, and we've had time to check through your inventory as well. Even identified the murder weapon, in fact.'

'Things are going well for you, then,' Eric said sourly.

'Oh, you could say that. Fact is, Ward, we've managed to fill in several of the blanks, so to speak. The scenario we're working on is that these two villains, they broke into Delamere Hall by way of a window at the back of the house . . . not too far from the butler's bedroom, but the guy was flat out. Too much cellar tipple, maybe, who knows? Anyway, they scouted around the ground floor, came upstairs, found the locked room and forced the door. Maybe they made some noise doing that, maybe Delamere was a light sleeper, anyway he came padding down from the floor above armed with a walking stick. Ex-Army, all that sort of stuff, instead of being sensible and ringing for help he decided to face the intruders.'

Charlie Spate shook his head, almost admiringly. 'Stupid old fool, but there you are . . .' He fixed Eric with a triumphant eye. 'Now you stated that the last time you saw the colonel, he was going over the inventory, and on the desk beside you was this wooden statuette. Heavy wood, you said it was—'

'Ebony.'

'That's it.' Charlie smiled. 'Well, turns out that was probably the murder weapon.'

Eric stared at him. 'You mean Colonel Delamere was struck down by the statuette?'

Spate nodded in self-satisfaction. 'They'd smashed the glass display case, were about to help themselves to the contents, Delamere came charging in on them, one of the villains took a swing at him with the statuette and . . . bang. The colonel went down, skull laid open, shard of bone into his brain, and traces of gold leaf . . .'

Eric was cold. 'They took the Anubis statuette with them.'

'Along with a few other things they grabbed hastily from the display case. They were in a hurry now, with the old man on the floor bleeding from the head. They scampered pretty quick, while the butler was dragging on his dressing gown at the back of the house. Not that he'd have given them much trouble . . . thing is, in their panicked haste they got careless.'

'They left traces,' Eric guessed.

'Exactly that. One of the guys scratched himself, reaching into the display case. Left a smear of blood.' Spate smiled happily. 'You know, Ward, I'm a great believer in what goes around, comes around. In a case like this, my faith in human nature is renewed.'

'How do you mean?' Eric asked warily.

'I believe . . . once a scumbag, always a scumbag. And I did warn you, Ward, I did warn you at the time.'

There was a cold feeling in Eric's stomach. He was beginning to guess where this was leading. 'Get on with it, DCI Spate,' he muttered.

'With great pleasure,' Spate replied, leaning forward with a smug grin on his lips. 'Like I said, I warned you that day in court. All right, Sam Macmillan and forensics buggered up the sample of DNA on that occasion, but the fact is we did have some DNA to play with. And now we got some more. And what do you think? The two samples match!'

'What are you saying?'

'The DNA belongs to our young friend Joe Fisher. We got this one dead to rights, Ward. There'll be no wriggling out of this for your young mate this time!'

He leant back in his chair, hooked one arm over its back.

The self-satisfied grin seemed to spread as he contemplated his enemy. 'Yep. Your mate Joe Fisher, he got away with that last charge, but on this one he doesn't stand a chance of running free. And you know what the nice thing is, Ward? If you hadn't got him off last time, he'd have had a short spell for burglary, handling stolen goods, that sort of stuff. But you got him off!'

Spate's tone hardened, and his eyes were suddenly cold. 'Now, it's different. This time, we'll have the bastard on a charge of murder!'

* * *

Jackie Parton was short, still lean, narrow-wristed and wiry of frame, as befitted an ex-jockey who had looked after himself and not run to fat on the good life. Not that Jackie's life had been particularly affluent, after the beating he had taken: various rumours had gone around about the reasons for the attack, but it had certainly ended his racing career. But not his fame. He was well known along the river, could count on numerous friends and acquaintances, and was well-placed for any gossip that might be rippling through the pubs and clubs and back alleys that clustered around the Tyne. There was some mystery about the manner in which he made a living but he had proved to be a useful friend to Eric Ward. Eric had known him in his racing days of course, and after he had finished his rides, and Eric had become a solicitor, Jackie Parton had proved to be a reliable informant. Eric paid him a retainer, and Jackie was always available to make use of his knowledge to seek out answers for Eric along the river.

It was to Jackie that Eric now turned.

He had explained about the relationship between Susie Cartwright and the young tearaway, and the ex-jockey had nodded in sympathy. He was fond of Susie anyway, and was only too willing to help try and find Joe Fisher. There was the added incentive that Charlie Spate was on the young man's trail.

'But this murder charge,' Jackie doubted. 'You think Spate'll make it stick?'

Eric shrugged. 'Let's find Fisher first. Let's hear his side of the story.'

'Will you act for him if he's charged?'

Eric hesitated. It was a difficult question to answer. He had not enjoyed the earlier experience of acting for Fisher: the man's arrogance and clear guilt of the crime he'd been charged with had left Eric ambivalent about his role. But he and Sharon Owen had done their duty by Fisher on that occasion: guilty or not he had been their client and they had acted in his best interests, if not those of justice. Now, if he was guilty . . .

The added complication was his secretary. Susie had turned pale when he had told her what Charlie Spate had said. 'Did you tell him—'

'Spate doesn't know he's your nephew,' Eric assured her.

She was shaken, and uncertain what to do. 'I don't want to make things difficult for you, Mr Ward. I should have spoken up sooner. And Joe Fisher is a bad lot, I don't doubt it. But murder . . . this will hit Jennie hard. But I don't think I can ask you to help him again—'

Eric had reassured her, albeit somewhat grimly. 'Let's not jump ahead of ourselves. We'll wait to find out where he's got to: I've asked Jackie Parton to make some enquiries. Once we get hold of Fisher, well, we can decide what needs to be done then, not before.'

But if Fisher had killed Colonel Delamere, Eric would be reluctant to take any part in his defence. There were too many conflicts of interests, and he had liked the old-worldly colonel. He hadn't deserved to meet such a brutal, unnecessary end. Meanwhile, all he could do was wait. At least Susie had cheered up somewhat, and though still a little subdued, at least she had become her usual effective self.

The rest of the week slipped past quickly. He managed to clear most of the urgent files from his desk, had two conferences with Sharon Owen on immigration matters in her chambers, where, she informed him mischievously, her colleague Featherstone could barely bring himself to speak to her. Late on Friday afternoon Eric told Susie he was leaving, and he returned to his flat in Gosforth to shower and change. He was surprised by the sense of nervous anticipation that again assailed him, at the prospect of spending the evening with Sarah Castle.

She appeared promptly at the Greek restaurant. He had come to expect it of her. Directness, punctuality, determination. She was an unusual woman. But very beautiful. She wore a figure-hugging dress with a decolletage he approved of. Her dark hair shone, she gave him a light kiss when he rose to greet her at the table and when she had ordered a gin and tonic for herself she looked at him, took his hands across the table, and asked him how his week had gone.

He burst out laughing.

'What's the matter?'

'You seem so . . . domesticated!'

'That's the first time that word has ever been used about me!' she complained.

'I didn't mean it as a criticism. It was just a bit unexpected. Sitting here, enquiring about my days. But, if you must know, things have gone pretty well. I've had a stack of work from the Foreign Office, and I've managed to get on top of it, so, I'm now free to enjoy my evening.'

Her glance slipped around the room, looking at the other clients in the restaurant. 'Or maybe even the weekend,' she murmured confidentially.

For some reason the thought of Sharon Owen brushed across his mind, the wings of a butterfly, but the touch was gone and he concentrated on the woman he was with. They talked: she told him anecdotes about her travels as a journalist, the odd people she had met, the eccentric editors she had had to deal with. They received their first course, had managed half of a bottle of wine, and then she suddenly stopped in mid-sentence, fell silent.

'What's the matter, Sarah?' he asked.

She managed a half-smile. 'I think this second visit to this restaurant might have been one too many. I fear we are about to be found out.'

Uncomprehending, Eric followed the direction of her glance. To his surprise, a man was standing up, leaving the table to which he had just been shown. He had a broad grin on his face, and he was making for their table.

'Neil Scanlon,' Eric moaned.

'The man himself,' Sarah muttered.

'Well, well, well,' Scanlon breezed, as he came over to them. 'The lawyer and the journalist. Do I detect a conspiracy here?'

'You're the theorist,' Sarah replied, and managed a welcoming smile that retained just a hint of asperity.

Scanlon seemed much himself, plump, confident, noisy but Eric felt he detected a certain hollowness about his eyes, forced bonhomie, a shadow in the man's welcome. Scanlon shook hands with him. 'Surprised to see you two here. Thought this place was one of my personal secrets. I come here most days. Favourite place to dine.' He beamed at them both. 'So what do you think of it?'

'We've been enjoying it, till now,' Sarah remarked, her winning smile removing the edge from her tone.

Scanlon hardly seemed to hear her. He was looking at Eric. 'I got your note. Haven't got around to answering. It was . . . kind of Jock to think of me in his will.'

He would find difficulty speaking of his old friend, Eric thought. He nodded his head. 'I thought I should let you have the details as they affected you. Though I fear a couple of the artefacts he left to you have disappeared, probably taken by the people who broke in.'

'Bastards!' Scanlon's pudgy features darkened. 'But at least Jock put up a fight. That was like him. As for the bits and pieces, I don't give a damn about them, as long as the police catch the evil thugs who are responsible.' He hesitated. 'Still, just came over to say hello. Didn't mean to intrude.'

For a moment, Eric felt sorry for the cocky little man. The death of Colonel Delamere would have shaken him. Sarah must have felt something similar because she asked, 'How's your work proceeding?'

'Work?' Scanlon repeated, almost blankly.

'The mysterious murder of the Lord Chancellor and his son.'

'Ah. My book.' Scanlon's brow cleared, and was immediately more at ease, some of his bantam arrogance returning. 'Let's say I'm following some new leads. Things are looking promising. I've got a new researcher, and she's come up with some interesting lines.'

'And what would they be?' Sarah Castle asked sweetly. Scanlon placed a hand on the back of the chair in front of him. He glanced at the empty place. 'If you don't mind, I'll sit down for a moment. Not to interrupt, of course, but . . .'

Eric opened his mouth to protest, glanced at Sarah, realised that she was about to make no objection and subsided.

Scanlon's tone was enthusiastic. 'I think you already know that after the tomb of Tutankhamun was opened, and the initial excitement had waned, things went sour for Carter. He had always had bad relations with Egyptian officials and interference increased from members of the Egyptian government in charge of archaeological exploration. Things got worse after the sudden death of Lord Carnarvon. Carter went to Luxor to meet the Minister of Public Works who told him that the digging concession was to be handed to Lady Carnarvon but only subject to official surveillance at the tomb, which Carter saw as malicious interference. There were two days of somewhat heated debate, during which Carter threatened to publish stories of their incompetence in the world's newspapers. Relationships deteriorated badly after that — Carter was well known for the short fuse he had on his temper and in December 1923 when the tomb entrance was locked, he really exploded.'

'He and his colleagues were locked out?' Sarah asked. 'What was Carter's response to that?'

'He was infuriated. He had done all the work, and now he was banned from continuing his excavations in the tomb except under supervision. For a short while as the nest surrounding the sarcophagus was removed, work continued while he fumed at what he saw as incompetent interference, but the final straw came when the concession to Lady Carnarvon was revoked in the following spring. Carter ordered his people to down tools by way of protest against the treatment they were getting from the Ministry of Public Works and the Antiquities Service.'

'That would hardly get him much further,' Eric surmised.

Sarah nodded. 'I seem to remember reading about that. Carter felt there was only one more course open to him.'

'Exactly,' Scanlon tapped the table with a confidential finger. 'He needed support. So, he made an appeal to the British Consulate at the Residency in Cairo.'

'How could they help?' Eric asked, glancing around to see if the waiter might intervene, bringing them their next course.

'Carter thought the High Consul, and the British Diplomatic Service, would be able to put pressure on the Zaghloul regime, to push them to give Lady Carnarvon a new concession. First, he tried General Allenby.'

'And?' Sarah leant forward, elbow on table, glanced at Eric and shook her head slightly.

'Unavailable. The unavailability might have been diplomatic. Anyway, Carter wasn't about to be dissuaded. He stormed the citadel himself. He marched straight into the Residency, met a high official there and harangued him about his grievances. The official expressed sympathy . . .'

In the pause, Eric guessed, 'But probably offered to do nothing.'

'In the way of all career-minded civil servants,' Scanlon sneered. 'That's about it. He made it clear the consulate could do nothing to influence the decisions of the Egyptian government or the Antiquities Service. Not within their jurisdiction, old boy.'

Eric could almost hear the man saying it. 'And Carter's reaction?' he asked, in resignation.

'This is where we get to the really interesting bit.' Scanlon leant back in his chair, and placed the tips of his fingers together. 'The official that Carter met has never been identified. Carter himself later described him as British Vice-Consul of Egypt. TGH James, in his book on Carter, says after consulting the Foreign Office List and Diplomatic Year Book for 1924 that it was one Captain TC Rapp. I have my doubts about that. But whoever the unnamed official might have been, we are able to state positively from Carter's diary notes that he had an appointment at the Residency on March 3rd 1924. That meeting turned out to be rather a torrid one.'

'I imagine Carter was incensed,' Sarah suggested. 'I read he always was a short-tempered man.'

'Apoplectic,' Scanlon agreed. 'And in the course of a violent argument he lost his temper, demanded that the British government intervene with the Egyptian authorities on his behalf. And he was not alone in his anger. It would seem that at the height of the . . . discussion . . . the unnamed official also lost his temper.' He paused, dramatically. 'He threw an inkwell at Carter's head.'

Eric's interest was aroused. He chuckled. 'He did *what*?'

'Threw an inkwell. Carter ducked, and the half-full inkwell bounced off the wall onto the carpet. It made quite a mess apparently.'

Sarah's eyes widened. 'Hardly diplomatic behaviour.' She paused, picked up her wineglass. 'Carter must have said something startling to cause such a reaction.'

Scanlon nodded. He seemed pleased with himself, recovering much of the verve and confidence that Eric had noted when they met at Delamere Hall. 'There's no record of what was actually said. But we can conclude from what happened that the official was incensed because Carter made some sort of threat.' He paused. 'We do know that the consular office walls had to be redecorated afterwards as a consequence of this . . . ah . . . disagreement.'

Eric was puzzled. 'A threat . . . On what grounds could Carter possibly threaten the British government?'

Scanlon eyed him owlishly, nursing a theory like a winning card held to his chest. 'Maybe he had some secret that he threatened to publish to the world.'

Eric sighed. He could guess what was coming. Scanlon was, after all, a conspiracy theorist. He glanced at Sarah. 'Now I wonder what that could be?'

'Whatever it was, it caused that quarrel . . . and then caused the officials to act in the manner that Carter had desired.' Scanlon paused, folding his arms in a self-satisfied manner. 'You see, not long afterwards, some kind of adjustment was made. Carter got his way. He went off on a highly successful tour of the United States and Canada, then returned to London while the British government worked out a suitable deal with the new Egyptian Prime Minister.'

'What sort of deal do you think that would that have been?' Sarah asked in a languid tone.

Scanlon looked smugly at them both. 'Carter and Lady Carnarvon formally renounced claims to treasures from the tomb; and a new clearance concession was granted — a one-year concession to Carter to work as archaeological agent on behalf of Lady Carnarvon. In fact, Carter then worked at the tomb for seven more years as chief excavator.'

'I'd love to have been a fly on the wall during that quarrel,' Sarah mused.

Eric was silent for a little while. He stared at Scanlon; the writer held Eric's gaze. He was expecting the question.

'All right,' Eric sighed. 'How does this link to the death of Richard Bethell and his father Lord Westbury?'

Scanlon beamed. 'That's the question I'm pursuing. But let me put it like this . . . Carter made some sort of threat. Later, the government did what he asked. And Carter gave something to the Bethells, for safe keeping.'

'Against what?' Sarah enquired.

Scanlon raised an eyebrow. 'Against its loss.'

'To whom?' Eric asked, finally catching the waiter's eye.

'One cannot be sure. Perhaps it was . . . foreign influences. Zealots. Fanatics. The church. The government.' Scanlon smiled faintly. 'You know how we conspiracy theorists work. We throw in all kinds of possibilities.'

'Even so, what evidence is there to suggest this . . . item was given to the Bethells?'

Scanlon leant forward, lowering his voice for effect. 'I believe it was the handing over of this item stolen from the tomb of Tutankhamun that later led to the mysterious fires that broke out in the Bethell home in Manchester Square in 1939; I am of the opinion that the search for the item led to the mysterious death of Richard Bethell; and later, in an attempt to either find the item, or perhaps to prevent it getting into circulation, Lord Westbury himself was killed.'

Eric stared at the man in the chair in front of him. The story he was hearing seemed fanciful, and so far supported by little evidence as far as he could ascertain. The waiter was at his elbow. He looked up. 'We'll have another bottle, please.'

Scanlon smiled, puffed out his cheeks. 'Forgive me. I'm a boring old fool. I'm intruding on your little tête-à-tête.'

Sarah Castle smiled. 'It was an interesting story, Mr Scanlon. I hope you'll find the answers you seek.'

'Oh, maybe, or maybe not. But there's a story for me there. And it'll sell. My editor is convinced of it. And who knows? My researcher and I, we might find the papers yet!'

'Papers!' Eric asked, in spite of himself.

'Oh yes, didn't I make that clear! We know Carter and his employer took various items from the tomb . . . faience, jewellery, bouquets and ankh candlesticks. Carnarvon himself later mentioned them to *The Times* special correspondent. But there was something else. I quote from his own words: *One of the boxes contains rolls of papyri* . . . But then, the strange thing is, everything afterwards goes quiet, until later, in 1923, after his bust-up at the Embassy, Carter wrote that there had been no papyri, merely rolls of linen, "probably loincloths". But can we believe Carter's word on the topic!'

'Why should we not!' Sarah Castle asked quietly.

Scanlon raised a cynical eyebrow and waved his hand in a dismissive gesture. 'Come, come, Miss Castle . . .' He stood up, one hand on the chair. 'Carter lied about so much else . . . as did Lord Carnarvon. The accounts of neither can be trusted because they are riddled with discrepancies. And I repeat, Carter's denial of the existence of the papyri came *after* his shouting match with the official in the British Embassy.'

Eric shook his head doubtfully, as the waiter approached with another bottle of wine. 'So what's your theory!'

Scanlon raised his pudgy nose and looked about him, almost as though he were sniffing the room for clues. 'Oh, I think that in spite of the denials of Carter and Lord Carnarvon, there were in fact papyri in the tomb; I think Carter and Carnarvon brought them out secretly and had them translated by their philologist, a man called Gardner. We don't know what was written in the papyri but my guess is that it was what was written there that caused the problem. It led to the extraordinary outburst at the British Embassy, when an inkwell was thrown at Carter's head by an infuriated civil servant.'

There was a short silence. Turning to leave them, Scanlon said casually, 'I think that after the scene at the Embassy, a promise was made to Carter. He then entrusted the bargaining counter — the papyri — to Richard Bethell, who was sympathetic to Carter. I think the idea was that Bethell was to hold them as a continuing threat in case the tomb continued to be closed to the excavators. Then, later, Carter was again given access to the tomb, he continued his work and that should have been the end of the matter.'

'But it wasn't!' Eric hazarded.

Scanlon shook his head. 'No. Carter had agreed not to expose the papyri, but he wasn't giving them up. But maybe someone discovered Richard Bethell's involvement and when he refused to hand them over, or denied their existence, that's why he died.'

Eric rolled his eyes at Sarah. She ignored him. 'And Lord Westbury?'

'There was later an outbreak of arson at Manchester Terrace. And then Lord Westbury himself plunged to his death.'

'But what could possibly have been in the papyri to bring about such mayhem?'

'That we may never know.' Scanlon backed away from them, to return to his own table. 'But it makes a good conspiracy theory, don't you think?'

Surprisingly, Sarah seemed reluctant to let him go. 'So what happened to the papyri after Westbury's death?'

'That's the big question. And one I'm still exploring. But I really must leave you now. It's time I placed my own order for dinner. Enjoy yourselves.'

After the cocky little man had returned to his own table, Eric puffed out his cheeks in amused exasperation. 'Remind me not to buy the book,' he requested.

* * *

At his apartment in Gosforth it happened very quickly. It was she who suggested they went there after dinner. Once at the flat, he was surprised at the swiftness with which she made her desire apparent. She undressed him and herself quickly; her fingers and lips were cool as they traversed his body; the lengthy, slow rituals in the darkness, as the two bodies learnt about each other, were a sensual delight; the rising of the passion that engulfed them was a wave of desire that left Eric stunned. That she was practised was obvious, that she desired him was clear, but he was surprised by the strength of his own passion.

During a pause in the warm darkness, she murmured. 'I think I'd better stay the night.'

He had no problem with that suggestion.

She left him after a while, while he dozed, seemingly spent, but when she returned to his bed her skin was cool, and its cold softness aroused him again.

He was still half asleep when she finally left him, showered, dressed quietly and kissed him lightly on the cheek.

'I'll be in touch,' she whispered.

He heard the door click lightly behind her.

CHAPTER 4

Jackie Parton was in touch with Eric on the following Monday morning. He suggested he and Eric meet that evening. He told Eric he might have some useful information.

After working on some of the Foreign Office files during the morning, Eric spent most of the afternoon at a packaging firm in Killingworth, discussing the issues arising from staff fraud and taking evidence from the company employees in the accounting department, regarding the unauthorised electronic transfer of funds that had been occurring for some months. Because of his appointment at Killingworth, Jackie Parton had suggested they meet at Union Quay, near the Shields Pedestrian Ferry: it would be easier to cross the river from there rather than drive through the Tyne Tunnel. Since the Killingworth business dragged on rather longer than he had anticipated, Eric was a little late for his meeting with the ex-jockey. He was also held up on the A19: a lorry had shed its load and the police had limited traffic to a single, crawling lane, slowed even further by the harsh, driving wind that had arisen, carrying a fine spray of rainwater against his windscreen.

As he chafed in the slow-moving traffic, Eric's thoughts turned back to his evening with Sarah Castle. To say that she had surprised him was an understatement. That they had been attracted to each other was obvious; she had been somewhat dilatory in making contact with him again since their first meeting, but once that contact had been made things had proceeded like wildfire.

Yet he was left with the vague feeling that it would be some time before she made contact once more. It was as though she was accustomed to keeping her life tightly packaged in compartments: work was one thing, socialising another, a love affair . . . He wondered whether that was what it was. He was uncertain about his own feelings. He had enjoyed being with her, their love-making had been an experience like none other, and the mere thought of her now made his body move again.

Practised, efficient, controlled. Was that really how she had been?

He was unsure.

It was just becoming dark when he pulled into the cobbled parking area opposite the imposing frontage of Collingwood Mansions, the former Seamen's Mission built alongside the river in North Shields. Jackie Parton's car was already there, but there was no sign of its owner. Eric could guess where he would find him, because only yards from the cobbled parking area was a pub called The Porthole. Eric locked his car, pulled up the collar of his raincoat against the whipping wind that was driving along the river and made his way into the side entrance of The Porthole. When Eric stepped through the doorway he had only a few moments to take in the flavour of the interior with its mock mainmast in the centre of the room, the Turks Head knots adorning the bar and the photographs and paintings of the nineteenth-century riverside scenes that hung on the walls. In the front room of the pub a jazz group was playing; the place was crowded. As Eric entered, Jackie was draining the dregs from his glass, rising to his feet, pulling on his donkey jacket.

'Ah, there you are. There's a ferry due, Mr Ward. We'd better get a move on, unless you're thirsting for a drink.'

'I can manage without,' Eric replied.

They left the pub immediately and made their way over the cobbled car park, past Collingwood Mansions, towards the old pub at the end of the lane, once called The Crane House. A sign proclaimed its new name — The Chain Locker — as part of its development into a block of flats. It was a reflection of what was happening all along the river from Whitley Bay to Wallsend, Eric mused. The old warehouses, graving docks, and rusting riverside paraphernalia, the detritus of long-disappeared industry, they were all giving way to housing developments and small business premises.

The wind hurried them, buffeted them down to the floating dock which lurched under their feet when they reached the ferry: the blue-and-white painted, newly launched *Spirit of the Tyne* waited for them, urgent to leave. The door closed behind them with a warning signal before they took their seats.

'Lot more comfortable than it used to be,' Jackie Parton grunted, looking about him appreciatively.

Darkness was falling on the river. The wind had risen sharply, violent white water danced and surged against the hull and a fine spray of mist rose as the ferry set off, turning into the wind, pausing while the sleek, towering, white and blue shape of the *Princess of Norway* ghosted its way past them, almost soundlessly it seemed, the overnight ferry headed out of the river on the crossing to Stavanger and Bergen.

'Nivver done that trip,' Jackie Parton mused thoughtfully.

'Neither have I . . . Who exactly are we going across to South Shields to meet?' Eric asked.

Jackie grimaced. 'Old mate of mine. Used to be a bookie, straight enough for one of them if you know what I mean. Retired from the business when the muscle moved in and it got too hard to stay independent. Never a hard man was Philly Fredericks. Cunning, mind. Sharp eye for a horse and a good bet.' He glanced at Eric and smiled slightly. 'And since he retired, well, like me he's kept his eyes open. He's one of those people who are like flypaper: information's always sort of buzzed around him, then stuck, so he's a useful guy to know.'

White water slammed against the bows of the ferry as it continued the brief crossing of the darkening water. They docked with a shudder. When they disembarked the wind seemed to have risen even further, tugging at them, pulling them towards the harbour walk. 'We go down towards the Old Custom House,' Jackie muttered, lowering his head against the wind.

There was no one else about on the river walk. Local people had more sense, Eric thought to himself, on an evening like this. Heads down, the two men made their way along to the area known as Mill Dam; when they reached the former Customs House, now redeveloped as a theatre and exhibition rooms, Jackie turned left, leading the way across the cobbled square towards Coronation Street. There were three pubs on the small rise: the first was the Steamboat Inn. Its windows gleamed with light, its external walls painted in faded dark red and dirty cream colours.

Warm air reached out to them as they entered. Eric had never been there before. He was taken aback by the sight that met him. The pub was divided into several small, timber-floored rooms beyond the bar, at different levels. Above the bar hung sepia-coloured photographs of ships that had been built on the Tyne in years gone by. The ceiling was festooned with a motley collection of ship's lanterns, pots, mugs, cast iron bells and harpoon irons. Jackie hesitated, glanced around the half-empty bar then turned, ascended a couple of steps into the next level, and then gestured with his hand.

'Philly,' he explained to Eric.

The walls of the room beyond the main bar were almost covered in photographs of the Tyne-built *Mauretania,* the various stages of its construction, its maiden voyage out of the river, diagrammatic plans of its decks. In the corner of the room, seated on a green velour-covered bench seat, in front of a display case dominated by an array of miniature bottles and a wild-eyed, bearded sailor's head — a miniature bottle of malt whisky clamped between his broken teeth — and directly under a series of wall-mounted clocks and ship's gauges, sat the man they had come to meet.

Philly Fredericks was perhaps sixty years of age. His hair was dyed black, slicked back smoothly; his features were narrow, careful, oddly unlined. He wore a casually knotted silk scarf around his neck, a white shirt and plain green tie, hound's-tooth jacket, sharp-creased, narrow black trousers and black socks. Incongruously, his shoes were of a white plastic. He rested his left hand on an ivory-knobbed wooden cane. His left eyebrow was cocked inquisitorially as he caught sight of Eric.

Jackie Parton stood in front of his old acquaintance.

After a brief silence he said, 'Blowing a hooley, outside.'

'Wild as the wife on washin' day,' Philly Fredericks agreed amicably enough.

'So what you up to these days?' Jackie asked, as he gestured to Eric to take a seat facing Fredericks.

The former bookmaker shrugged thin shoulders in his hound's-tooth jacket. 'Like always. Wife-swappin' parties.'

'How did you get on?' Jackie asked.

'Got an old bike in return for the missus. But it was a disappointin' swap.'

'Why's that?' Jackie asked, shrugging out of his donkey jacket.

'It had a flat tyre.'

Jackie grunted, winked at Eric. 'The old jokes are always the best,' he muttered. He began to make his way to the bar, calling out over his shoulder to Philly Fredericks. 'Pint of Black Sheep do for you?'

'Nicely.'

Eric settled for a half of cider; the old familiar ache had started at the back of his eyes and he was unwilling to cause any further problems. The drugs he took nowadays had reduced the problem significantly, but there were still times when the old, cat-scratching claws came back, tearing away at the back of his eyes. He sat quietly in the seat opposite Philly Fredericks, who eyed him carefully.

'Don't I know you from somewhere?'

'We've never met,' Eric replied.

'You a friend of Jackie's,' Fredericks ruminated. 'So you can't be polis.'

Eric shook his head. 'I'm a lawyer.'

Fredericks was unimpressed, and was not averse to showing it. He sniffed disdainfully. 'Just as bad, really.' He considered the matter for a few seconds, watching Eric carefully. 'So you from across the river?'

'No. Newcastle.'

'Ha, just as well. I hear they eat their own kids over there in North Shields.' Having delivered himself of the information, Fredericks was silent for a little while, staring indifferently at his empty glass, two hands grasping the ivory-topped cane. Eric noticed it was yellowish in colour, and had been carved. Fredericks saw him inspecting it. He removed one hand, to show the features of a wild-eyed, long-tressed sea witch. 'Scrimshank,' he announced loftily. 'Came off a whaler in the old days: seamen used to spend months, while they was at sea, carving these pieces of ivory. Or whalebone. Or whatever.' He eyed Eric craftily. 'Covered in blood, it was, when I acquired it. Man got his head beaten in with it, at Newcastle Races.'

Eric didn't believe it and was disinclined to ask the obvious questions. Philly Fredericks, tall-tale teller, was clearly a little put out. In the awkward silence that followed, Eric looked about him at the photographs of the *Mauretania,* the tidal charts of the river from St Anthony's Point to Dunston, the glass case with a seaman's bearded head, the pile of ancient, dusty encyclopaedia on the window sill. Jackie returned carrying a small tray with the drinks and slid into the seat beside his old acquaintance.

'Got to know each other then?'

'You might say that,' Eric remarked drily.

Jackie Parton turned to the old man. 'Don't get to Gosforth Park these days, then?'

Fredericks grunted sourly. 'Races are over for me. Stay south of the river mostly. Know most of the villains this side, so can stay out of the way when there's trouble.' He sipped at his glass of Black Sheep and grimaced in satisfaction. Wiping a line of froth from his lips with a lean, fastidious finger he looked at Jackie. 'So your friend's a lawyer, then,' Fredericks commented. 'Slummin' it south of the river, comin' over to see the sand dancers.'

'Sand dancers?' Eric asked, puzzled.

Philly Fredericks bared his teeth. 'Why aye, man. Been told, haven't you? Place around here, Mill Dam, Laygate, it's always been full of them sand dancers, seamen from overseas, Moslem Arabs mainly. The sand dancers, they been around South Shields more than a while. Story is they been comin' to the Mill Dam for a hunnerd years or more: they hired as seamen, got discharged in Laygate, then used to pick up another boat to ship out. That was in the old days of coal and shipbuildin' on the Tyne. Always been quite a settlement of them around here. Used to bunk in lodgings run by other Arabs, and then later they set up their own businesses. They still got a mosque up at High Shields, and there's a Yemeni School right next door to it.'

'There was trouble a while back, wasn't there?' Jackie asked. 'I seem to remember . . .'

'Aye, you might have read about it but it was a bit before your time. The big trouble was in the thirties. In the big Depression there was a few riots down here at Mill Dam. Quite a number of the sand dancers had settled down by that time, with local women . . . and that caused some bother, you can imagine. The locals reckoned they always got the best-looking girls. Well, they was good-looking buggers, wasn't they?' He glared fiercely at Eric, as though challenging refutation.

'Anyway, like I said, in time the sand dancers, they picked up more stable jobs, had families, settled down. But they still stayed among their own groups . . . Arabs, mainly, or Somalis. It was cos of them Arabs that we had so many curry houses down along Ocean Road.' A hint of pride crept into his tone. 'It's cos of them sand dancers that we got the most curry houses in one strip in the north! Still about seventeen in a hunnerd yards. Tandooris they call themselves now. But over the years, what with the Mill Dam area being redeveloped, most of them moved away from Laygate, up onto the new housing estates at Cleadon and Harton. Still not too far from their mosque, of course. Walkin' distance, like.' He took a hefty swallow from his pint glass, eyed Jackie Parton carefully. 'But all I'm doing is givin' you local colour, hey? I don't really suppose it's the sand dancers you wanted to talk about, is my guess.'

Jackie nodded slowly. 'Aye, well, that's right. My friend here . . .'

'The lawyer.'

'Yes, that's right. Well, he's been acting for a young scallywag who I hear spent a fair bit of time south of the river. I thought you might be able to help us with him . . . where we might find him, who he's been hanging out with, that sort of thing. His name's Joe Fisher.'

Philly Fredericks bared stained teeth. 'Fisher? Right villain that one. Cocky little bastard. Knows it all, or thinks he does. Aye, I know of young Joe Fisher. He'll likely find hisself bottom of the river one of these days.' He glanced at Eric, shook his head. 'You can see these young scum a mile off, when they're growin'. It starts with petty stuff, nickin' the odd bit of stuff, moves onto twockin' cars to order, then they get the swagger, flash the money around . . . I've seen him around here often enough. Loud mouth. Louder since he got tied up with that bastard Jag Thomas.'

'Who might he be?' Jackie asked quietly.

'Fancies himself as a ringmaster, does Jag,' Philly Fredericks sneered. 'Red-haired bugger. Story is, he never gets directly involved himself: butters up these young thugs, sets them up to do jobs so the risk is all theirs, and then fences what they bring in. Direct descendant of that there Fagin, if you ask me. But more vicious. He don't usually do the business in the break-ins and that, but he's not backward comin' forward with a six-inch blade.'

'What sort of seam is he involved in these days?' Eric asked.

Philly Fredericks shrugged in disdain. He twiddled his cane top in his fingers. 'They say he's been smugglin' cigarettes in on lorries dischargin' off the freighters comin' in from Europe. My own bet is he's got his mucky fingers onto drugs, though.'

'And Joe Fisher is involved in this business?'

Philly Fredericks frowned, thought about it for a little while. 'Not sure about that. Jag Thomas, he's got a system, you see. Gets 'em involved young, trains 'em up. He's headin' that way, mind. I hear Fisher's been on the transport run.'

'What do you mean?' Jackie asked.

'You know . . . straight enough stuff to start with. There's a group of these youngsters, they pick up casual work drivin' cars off and on the freighters. As the big boats come in, dump their loads and then start pickin' up a cargo of new cars for shippin' to Africa or what have you, the agents need casual labour, half of them bloody twockers if you ask me, to drive the cars up on the boat, stack up neat, that sort of thing.'

'It sounds legitimate work to me,' Eric doubted.

'Course it is,' Fredericks agreed. 'But it brings in the contacts, don't it? There's seamen on those boats, crew who ship from port to port. Easy to slip stuff to these young lads: no Customs inspection, after all, because they got to move fast, get the cars on to catch the next tide.' He nodded wisely. 'It's just an early step for the kids. Fisher's been doin' that for a while . . . but then, as we know, he was movin' on to other things for Jag Thomas, like that burglary a few months back . . .' His eyes flicked up suspiciously to Eric. He frowned, puzzled. 'You said you was a lawyer.'

'It was Mr Ward who got young Fisher off,' Jackie intervened.

'And now he ain't paid you, that it?' Fredericks grinned. 'Doubt you'll ever see your money from that one. Not now he's in with Jag Thomas.'

The wind outside seemed to have gained in intensity. There was a brief howling noise, a call of complaint as the side door to the bar was opened and someone entered. A stocky man in a leather jacket appeared at the foot of the steps that led up to the snug where Fredericks was holding court. He glanced at them briefly, ran a hand over his damp, fair, close-cropped hair, strolled into the room where they sat, looked around in a desultory fashion at the *Mauretania* photographs on the wall and then wandered back into the bar. He had his back to them, ordering himself a whisky.

'So where do you reckon we'll find this precious pair, Fisher and his mentor Thomas?' Jackie asked.

Fredericks wrinkled his nose. 'There's a nightclub down near the Tyne Dock. It's convenient for the loadin' areas. It's known as a good place to do business. Of the shady kind, I mean. As far as I know, Fisher's got an apartment in that area, too. My bet is that's where you'll find him . . . if he's not off on a job for Thomas.'

'You know where his apartment is in the area?'

'Think it's in a block called Venture Point House. I hear that's where he comes and goes. Not very wise, if you ask me.'

'Why's that?'

Philly Fredericks leant forward, thumped his cane on the wooden floor of the snug. There was a woman behind the bar, heavy-breasted, turning to fat, hair tinted a shocking pink. She looked up, caught Frederick's eye and nodded. The man who had recently come in did not turn his head. He finished his whisky, and walked away from the bar. The wind whistled briefly at his exit, then died again as the door slammed shut.

'In a hurry, that one,' Fredericks observed. 'Downed that whisky in two shakes.'

'You said it wasn't very wise for Fisher to live at Venture Point,' Jackie urged.

'Oh, aye. Well, you got to realise the old ways take a long time to die down. The curry houses up in Ocean Road now, well, they're sort of westernised if you know what I mean.

The buildin' contractors, the young men comin' out of the pubs at night, they all go down there for a late curry. Always sure of gettin' one. But Venture Point, well, it's still a sand dancer area. I mean, these guys can be territorial. Fact is, the older generations have settled down, got jobs in Newcastle, or Shields or Durham . . . but a lot of the youngsters, they're just drifters. Like all young kids. The papers call them disaffected . . . Load of bollocks, if you ask me. They're just like the white lads. Look out for trouble, a quick handful of tenners here and there, and maybe a punch-up on a Saturday night. Or any night, come to that. And it's not fists these days,' he added mournfully. 'It's knives, innit?' He shook his head. 'Naw, if I was young Joe Fisher, I'd move away from them flats. Too much stuff goin' on.'

The blowsy barmaid left the bar and made her way up to the snug. She was carrying a pint glass of Black Sheep in her hand. She set it down in front of Philly. 'On the house, this time. As an old regular,' she said, smiled, and went out.

'I think she fancies you,' Jackie Parton said.

Philly Fredericks sniffed disdainfully. 'I'd rather have a packet of crisps.'

* * *

The rain had arrived. It swept along from Coronation Street and battered against the doorway of the Steamboat Inn. The two men stood huddled in the meagre shelter provided by the doorway, peering out into the street. 'So what do you think?' Eric asked.

'I don't know, Mr Ward. If the polis is now after Joe Fisher, as you think is the case, chances are he'll have scampered from his lodgings. And I don't think he'll spend too much time hangin' around at Tyne Dock either, loadin' them cars. But one thing's for sure. He won't lose contact with the guy who sets up the jobs for him.'

'Jag Thomas?'

Jackie nodded. The wail of a siren came from the river. Above the roar of the buffeting wind they caught another siren sound: police cars, more than one of them, charging their way along the road behind them. There was a flickering of lights, blue and red, bouncing starkly off the walls down at the Mill Dam. 'Something's up,' Jackie observed quietly.

Eric had other things on his mind. 'I don't know there's much we can do . . . if it wasn't for Susie's involvement . . .'

'I can try to sniff around a bit more this side of the river,' Jackie suggested. 'Maybe even get something from this Thomas character. I got friends over here . . . they might be able, to be a bit persuasive, make Thomas see the error of his ways. It might lead us to Fisher.' He paused, eyed Eric in the driving darkness. 'If you get hold of him, what you going to do?'

Eric shook his head. 'Get his side of the story. Probably try to get him to turn himself in, take his chances. A lot depends on whether he can explain how his DNA appeared at Delamere Hall.'

'We all know the answer to that one,' Jackie grunted cynically. 'But, I suppose for the sake of Susie Cartwright, we better try to do what we can for the young bugger . . .' He had raised his chin, almost as though he was sniffing the wind for trouble. 'You hear that, Mr Ward?'

'What?'

'Another police siren. Somethin's goin' on, down at Tyne Dock I reckon.' He hesitated, looked about him. 'Look, Mr Ward, there's nothin' more you can do down here tonight. There's a ferry crossing in ten minutes. You get down there, make your way back to Newcastle. I'll be in touch again as soon as I got more.'

'What are you going to do now?' Eric asked doubtfully.

'There's somethin' up. I can sense it, like. But you don't want to get involved with anythin' over here. Leave it to me. I'll be in touch.'

Jackie Parton nodded goodbye, hunched into his donkey jacket, and Eric watched the small figure of the man hurrying away down the street towards Mill Dam. The wind plucked at him, urged him sideways, pushed him against the walls. Then he was lost to view in the driving, gusty rain.

* * *

It was not that Charlie Spate was unused to working in bad, wet, windy weather. It was just that in his view the rain down south had always been kinder, softer, more accommodating, and when it was really bad there had usually been a warm bed he could creep into, get solace from a whore who owed him, stay out of the way until trouble and bad weather died down.

Up here it was different.

The rain seemed to bear a perpetual grudge against southerners. It whistled in your face, got down the back of the neck, seemed to take a perverse satisfaction in gusting particularly at men who didn't belong up here in the north-east. And there were no available beds. Well, they were available, he guessed, but since it was his reputation for sailing close to the wind with whores and villains that had led him to take the recommended transfer out of the Met, he'd felt it best to stay away from such temptations. Which was one reason why he had lusted after Elaine Start for so long. He'd have given a great deal to be in her bed right now. He wondered where she was.

Not on this benighted operation, that was for sure.

Charlie saw absolutely no reason why he should be on this side of the river at all. He'd had it out with Charteris.

The assistant chief constable had briefed him in his office. 'Macmillan is still acting as liaison on the south shore, but you're his senior officer so I think you'd better get over there on a watching brief. It looks as though they could be wrapping it all up tonight. The South Tyne lads are in full order, and Major Cryer will be there too. I don't want us to be seen to be dragging our feet. So I want you there.'

'Sir—'

'They go in early evening,' Charteris snapped. 'I would have advised an early morning operation as usual, but Cryer informs me that from the information they've received the subject will be present in Venture Point block of flats around about 7 p.m. The idea is to grab him then. If he slips the net, there's no telling which way he'll head. It's a golden opportunity. So Cryer reckons.'

'So the major says so,' Spate commented bitterly, 'and we all jump.'

Charteris fixed him with a cynical eye. 'You still don't seem to get the message, Charlie. We've all got our instructions. Me, I have to do what the Chief says. The Old Man himself, well, I know he's under a directive from the Home Office and the bloody Foreign Office as well! With bloody MI6 thrown in.'

'Military intelligence,' Charlie snarled. 'Where are they getting their information from anyway, getting us charging up our own arses—'

'You heard me say it,' Charteris said coldly. 'We're doing as we're told. All of us. And you . . . you'll be across the river at South Shields this evening.'

'In the bloody weather,' Charlie said unhappily. 'There's a storm forecast.'

'You made of sugar, so you'll melt?' Charteris asked contemptuously.

* * *

The young police constable standing beside Charlie was nervous: he looked to be in his early twenties and Charlie guessed this was his first operation. Charlie didn't know him: he was attached to the South Tyneside group. He was burly enough, and looked even bigger with the flak jacket he was wearing. Cryer was clearly expecting trouble.

'I only been on the force couple of weeks,' the young man muttered. 'Grew up around here, like: down Ocean Park way. But family moved to Derby so I did my last schooling there. Allus wanted to get back though.' He grimaced, glanced out at the sweeping rain. 'Don't ever remember it being this wet, though.'

Charlie was unconvinced.

Major Cryer was standing across the room, near the door. He'd already given the briefing: it was clear just who was in charge of this operation. Sam Macmillan looked tense; he glanced up, caught Charlie's eye, and licked his lips.

Cryer checked his watch. 'Five minutes,' he intoned. 'Right, we can start to take up our positions.'

Charlie had arrived late for the briefing but knew more or less what was going down. He'd done it all before, with larger groups than this, during his days in the Met. The target was Venture Point, and the block of flats on the rising hill that gave a view over the town, with glimpses of the river mouth. On a good day, Charlie thought sourly.

They had split into three units: as an observer Charlie would be going in with the second wave, once the first group — led by the South Tyneside armed intervention unit — had pounded their way into the designated flat. Charlie hoped they'd get it right. He'd seen enough cockups in the past to know that this could go badly wrong . . . particularly if a wanker like Major Cryer was in charge. Charlie had little confidence in the man. To start with, the MI6 officer was running down the wrong road. It wasn't this Ismail Badur character they should be concentrating on. It was Joe Fisher they wanted.

But he guessed Major Cryer had an agenda of his own.

This wasn't really about Fisher, or Delamere, or anything else to do with villains on the South Tyne: it was field officers doing their spook bit. Charlie's lip curled in disgust. This was not something he wanted to be part of.

The minutes ticked past. The tension in the room was rising, men fiddling with the harness of their flak jackets, nervous muttering, a clearing of dry throats. Cryer raised his head. In a quiet tone he said, 'Right, let's go.'

Charlie hung back as he'd been directed.

The first four men slipped out of the room. When they opened the door the wind whipped rain in their faces; with lowered heads they ran across the courtyard to the shelter of

142

the doorway leading into the side entrance to the vestibule of the apartment block. Charlie waited with the others. The first group disappeared; the group leader with Charlie was staring at his watch. Cryer had insisted this was to be handled like a military operation. Charlie wondered just how much field experience the MI6 officer had obtained.

'OK. Let's go!'

Charlie followed the second group as they rushed around to the side door: the third group of officers would by now have secured the front entrance. When Charlie dashed through the rain his group were already inside the vestibule, spreading out. Somewhere someone screamed, and as the heavy boots pounded on the stairs all hell seemed to break out. There was the sound of a door being smashed in on the first floor: a terrified woman crouched against the wall on the first bend of the stairway; below him Charlie could see two grim-faced officers taking up position at the entrance to the lift.

Charlie's blood was up as he ran up the stairs. The officers were making as much noise as they could: shouting commands, yelling, creating a disorientating pandemonium, deliberately attempting to confuse their quarry. As Charlie skidded into the corridor he saw the officers pouring into the target area; the door sagged on its hinges, there was a sudden gust of smoke, an explosive sound, and an acrid smell hit Charlie's nostrils, caught the back of his throat.

Charlie had been in better organised operations, but none as noisy. Worse, he could understand almost nothing that was being shouted. Northern accents filled the air: excited, scared men yelling, not knowing what to expect.

A door opened down the hall; a black man stuck his head out. His eyes were wide and terrified. Someone screamed at him to get back inside but he seemed not to understand. He stepped out, half-crouching, looking as though he was about to run. Reason prevailed. He turned, shot back into his room like a startled rabbit, slammed the door behind him.

Charlie followed his own group into the apartment. Two bedrooms, they'd been told, a sitting room, kitchen, bathroom, corridor leading through to the back. He checked the corridor: the window at the rear had been smashed and there was an officer standing there, staring out, his upper body leaning into the driving rain. From the plans they'd looked at there would be a sheer drop back there; anyone legging it out that way would probably end up with a broken leg or ankle in the darkness. Charlie turned, stepped into the sitting room.

It was a shambles. Acrid smoke curled around the ceiling light. Chairs and a settee had been overturned, a table lamp smashed on the threadbare carpet. Huddled against the wall was a woman; Charlie guessed she was in her thirties. Her large, liquid eyes held no trace of fear as she crouched, harangued by Cryer in a language that Charlie did not recognise. He guessed it was Arabic. Cryer was spitting out the words, his face contorted with fury. The woman stared at him, unflinching, a hint of contempt in her manner. Cryer balled his fist in frustration, and for a few seconds Charlie thought he was going to hit her. But the MI6 man held back, controlled himself as a great bull elephant of a man blundered into the room, menacing in helmet and flak jacket. Another officer followed him, shoving two young men in their twenties ahead of him. One of them had a rapidly swelling left eye, and he was yelling blue murder. It might have been Geordie but it could have been pure Arabic as far as Charlie was concerned: he didn't understand a word. The other man, a curly haired, olive-skinned individual was in more control, but there was fury in his eyes as he caught sight of the woman crouching against the wall. He directed a glance full of venom at Cryer.

The helmeted bull elephant shouted at Cryer. 'Other rooms cleared, sir! These are all we got!'

The veins of smoke curled languidly above their heads. Cryer bared his teeth in a vicious grimace of disappointment. He was about to say something when he twitched, fumbled inside his jacket and pulled out a mobile phone. Charlie heard the faint buzz. Cryer checked the caller, then lifted the phone to his ear, marched out towards the doorway. He muttered something briefly, then listened. A frown came onto his face, his brows knitting in thought. He snapped the phone shut, looked back at Charlie. 'Hold on here. I'll be back.'

He disappeared down the stairwell. Charlie stood in the room with the two flak-jacketed policemen, the two young men and the woman. The man with the bruised face stood back against the wall, his companion went forward to the woman, spoke rapidly to her. The bull elephant pushed himself between them, angrily. For a moment Charlie thought there was going to be trouble, but the woman shouted something, and the edge went from the two youths. They lolled back against the wall, waiting, as another two officers entered the room. Then they all stood around uncertainly, muttering amongst themselves, uncertain what the next step was to be, waiting for Cryer's return.

It was his word clearly; he was in charge of the whole operation. And now he had disappeared. Charlie shook his head. What a cock-up! And it was clear that the man they'd come looking for — this Ismail Badur — he was certainly not around. And, Charlie had no doubt, Cryer would get nothing out of the fish he'd caught in his feeble net.

He gritted his teeth. The resources that were being wasted on this wild goose chase for the so-called terrorist . . . it was Joe Fisher they should be out looking for. Or he should, at least: his presence here on the south bank of the Tyne was just a complete waste of time. Charlie stayed there, cooling his heels for several minutes. He wandered out into the corridor, stared down the stairs. There was an officer down there, bored: he'd lit up a cigarette. If Cryer caught him at that, Charlie considered, there'd be high words. The thought stirred him and he went down to join the copper, cadged a cigarette from him — it was a long time since Charlie had had a drag, but what the hell.

The apartment block was still noisy. Not the thundering of boots or the harsh shouting of the attack force, but the chattering of birds, the murmuring of bees, people poking their heads out of windows and doors, calling out enquiries, wondering what the hell was going on. He looked out himself. The rain was still lashing down, and there seemed to be flashing blue lights everywhere. Cryer seemed to have called out half the police cars on the force.

But oddly, two of them, roaring past, were headed down the hill, towards the river. Charlie hesitated, wondering about that. The operation here was a failure; Cryer seemed to have disappeared God knows where, and squad cars were hurrying down the hill, towards the Tyne Dock. The crackling of static from the walkie-talkies filled the air. There was a lot of chat going on.

A flak-jacketed officer slouched in from the rain, stopped at the foot of the stairs, swearing. Charlie heard what he muttered to his companion. 'While we're messin' about here that Major Cryer, he's slipped out for a pint!'

'You what?'

'One of the lads in a squad car just saw him, stoppin' off in the Steamboat.'

Charlie turned towards the officer, just stubbing out his cigarette nervously. 'What's that you said?'

'Well I dunno, sir. I mean, someone just said—'

Bollocks to this for a party, Charlie thought. He'd had enough. He hesitated, glared out at the rain-swept night. Cryer had told him to hang on, but he was there on observation and not strictly subject to Cryer's commands, MI bloody 6 or not. And Macmillan, where the bloody hell was Macmillan? He was the liaison officer — why wasn't he at his post? Maybe in the bloody pub with Cryer!

Charlie stamped around in the tiled vestibule for a few minutes, angrily. Then he made up his mind. To hell with Operation Cryer. His nose sniffed something; there was too much activity outside in the road, running down to Tyne Dock. Cursing, he ran out into the rain; a squad car was just pulling out from a side street. Charlie ran towards it, waving. He dragged out his warrant card. Reluctantly, the driver allowed him to climb into the back seat.

He was on his way to the river. That suited Charlie. He wanted to know what the hell was going on.

They reached the roundabout and swung into the river road. Ahead of them the derricks shone with bright lights; to the left a freighter was in the process of loading cars, but there were people standing around, huddled in the rain: the line of cars had stopped. The radio crackled in the car. They swept past the freighter, headed out towards the dock.

There were several squad cars ahead of them, lights flashing. A small crowd had gathered, crewmen, it looked like, workers from the docks. They were held back by several constables. Charlie got out of the car, pushed through the crowd. As he did so they parted, letting him through. One of the crowd, a small, lean figure huddled in a donkey jacket turned to look at Charlie: the blue flashing light lit up his features for an instant, and Charlie experienced a moment of recognition. Then the man had faded into the crowd and Charlie ploughed on, dismissing the thought as he headed down across the Quayside.

Warrant card in hand he marched down to the edge of the jetty. There was a small knot of officers there, two of them crouching over a dark form on the ground. A radio crackled; behind him, in the distance Charlie heard the siren wail of an ambulance. As he approached the group he heard one of the officers say, as he jerked his head towards the sound of the approaching ambulance, 'Fat lot of good that'll do.'

Charlie pushed forward. 'What's going on?'

'Fished a stiff out of the water.'

'Is that unusual?' Charlie grunted.

'We get a few, from time to time. But with all that's been going on tonight . . . Call came in when we were all on stand-by.'

'Man or woman?'

'Man.' The officer stepped aside willingly as Charlie edged forward. He was now standing at the edge of the group. One of the crouching officers stood up, shaking his

147

head. 'That's about all we can do for this poor bastard. Let forensics have him now. They on their way?'

It was Sam Macmillan. He must have stepped in as senior officer. The South Tyneside coppers were all elsewhere, chasing wild Arabian geese.

'Mac! What you got?'

'Hello, Charlie. Thought you was up with Cryer.'

'Where *you* were supposed to be,' Charlie countered. 'So what's all this?'

'Stiff. Piled up against the jetty. No one around with any rank so I came on down here.'

'He been dead long?'

Macmillan shook his head doubtfully. 'I'm no pathologist, but I don't reckon he'll have been dead more than an hour or so. But you ought to see this.'

He stepped aside so Charlie could take a better look. The view was not a pleasant one. The corpse was lying on its back, fully clothed, long reddish hair twisted and tangled, the face a bluish-white under the lights, eyes wide open, staring blankly upwards.

The face had taken a severe battering. The nose was twisted out of shape, the left ear seemingly almost torn off. But what attracted Charlie's attention was the throat. The wound in the throat was horrendous. It gaped blackly, leaving the head to sag at an odd angle.

Macmillan grunted. 'Almost severed the head from the body.'

Charlie felt his gorge rise. He stepped back, breathed deeply. He raised his face to the black sky. The rain was easing. He glanced at Macmillan. 'Not really our business,' he said.

Macmillan shrugged. 'I'm walking away from this as soon as one of their own can take over. It's a mess we're well out of, Charlie. What's happening up at Venture Point?'

'It's a joke. Drawn a blank. The bird had flown the coop before we arrived. If he was ever bloody well there at all. What a bloody night.'

Macmillan turned his head, away from Charlie. 'What was that you said?'

He was addressing one of the local officers, who had said something to one of his colleagues.

'I was just saying, Sarge. Can't be sure, seeing that stiff the way he is, but I got a feeling I know him.'

'You recognise the man?'

'Think so . . .' An edge of doubt had crept into the man's voice. He turned, peered over a shoulder to look at the limp body on the jetty again. 'Local villain. Well enough known, though we never got a glove on him for most of the stuff he's pulled. Spends a lot of time at the night club, just up the road there. He's what you might call a percentage player. He's the puppet-man. Pulls the strings.'

'So what's he called?'

The officer hesitated. 'If I'm right . . . from what I can see . . . I mean, he didn't walk around with a throat like that, did he?' When no one sniggered, he shrugged. 'I think it's a character called Thomas. Runs scams this side of the river. Mainly off the freighters, but got a hand in most of the minor mucky stuff. Thomas. Yeah, I reckon that's who it is. Or was.' He shrugged his shoulders, nodded, convincing himself. 'That's right. He's called Jag Thomas.'

* * *

It was nothing he could actually put his finger on.

He woke in the night and listened to his own measured breathing in the darkness, and there were no other sounds to disturb him, nothing unusual or out of the ordinary. At work he found his mind drifting, as he stopped working, listened, looked about him, disturbed by something he could not define.

When he got into his car he sat behind the steering wheel and remained still for several seconds, something dark fluttering at the back of his mind. And when he got out, locked the vehicle and walked from the underground car park in Dean

Street to his office on the Quayside he paused, looked over his shoulder, unable to determine just what was making him uneasy and yet wary, edgy, imbued with the feeling that he was being followed; someone was watching his every move.

It was an odd sensation, an unpleasant one, but there was little rationality about it. He saw no one following him, heard nothing unusual, and yet all the time he felt that there was someone at his shoulder, observing his every move.

His edginess was not assuaged when he discovered that DCI Charlie Spate was waiting for him in the anteroom to his office. Susie, stiff-backed, was behind her desk getting on with her work. Spate sat silently, staring at his hands.

'You wanted to see me again?' Eric asked in a surly tone.

'That's why I'm here.'

Reluctantly Eric nodded towards his office. 'You never seem to be away. You'd better come in.'

Spate followed him into the office and took a seat without invitation. He watched as Eric pushed some files aside and sat down behind his desk. 'We pulled a body out of the river last night. On the south shore.'

'Indeed.'

Charlie Spate raised his head suspiciously. 'You don't seem surprised.'

'I was at South Shields last night. Near the Mill Dam. There was a lot of activity . . . police cars dashing around. I'm assuming it might have been something to do with that.'

Spate was silent for a little while. Eric waited. 'Whoever did for the stiff wasn't messing around. Still, when thieves fall out . . .'

* * *

Naturally, it was not the theory held by Major Cryer. There had been a quick debriefing, near midnight. The identity of the dead man had been established quickly: the officer who had spoken to Charlie had been quite right.

'So they must have had a right falling out,' Charlie suggested.

Major Cryer, Charteris and Macmillan had stared at him. 'Who?' Charteris asked.

'Joe Fisher.'

When the others said nothing Charlie went on, 'Well, stands to reason, doesn't it? He was a so-called mate of Jag Thomas. I think it was those two who did the burglary up at Delamere Hall. But Jag Thomas may have got greedy . . . or else Fisher turned on the guy who's been running his show for him. From what I hear it's Thomas who's been the dominant one. Maybe Fisher got fed up being ordered around. So they quarrelled, maybe over the loot, and Fisher laid into him.'

'It's a theory,' the man with the short-cropped hair muttered dismissively. 'But we're here to discuss the failure of the operation to capture Ismail Badur, not—'

'The failure,' Charlie cut in, blood staining his face, 'is down to poor intelligence work if you ask me. How the hell you expected to get the man you're after in the early evening, storming in like a bunch of cavalry troopers, escapes me. There was too much chance of it all going wrong. Too many people around to see things, make a guess what was going to happen, send out some warning signals.'

'We knew Ismail Badur was going to be there at that time,' Cryer insisted.

'But the bugger wasn't, was he? No disputing that! All you got was a woman with ice in her eyes and a couple of young layabouts—'

'They're part of the cell,' Cryer snapped.

'But I bet they won't be saying a word!' Charlie flashed back. 'If these guys are as organised as you claim they are, you could be working on them for months before you get anything out of the sneaky bastards!' He turned to Charteris in appeal. 'We wasted enough time on all this, sir. We got evidence that Joe Fisher was up at Delamere Hall; he was a close acquaintance, to say the least, of Jag Thomas; Fisher and Thomas are known to have used that area around Tyne Dock as their stomping ground, that night club as their business premises. In my opinion we got enough to bring Fisher in. Let's do something we got a chance of succeeding at, instead of standing around watching while bloody MI6 pursue their own agenda!'

Charteris didn't like it, partly, Charlie guessed because he was of the same view as Charlie. But he was under orders. 'Our instructions are to lend whatever assistance we can to Major Cryer. The investigation into the activities of Ismail Badur is on-going, and that means we—'

He was interrupted by Cryer. Charteris didn't like that either, Charlie noted.

'So you think that this man Thomas died at the hand of your suspect Fisher,' Cryer suggested coldly.

'He's an *obvious* suspect, because of the reasons I've already given.'

'Thomas was beaten badly.'

'They fell out! He and Fisher had a set-to!'

'It was more than a set-to, as you put it,' Cryer asserted. He paused. 'It looks as though Thomas was tortured before he died.'

Charlie was shaken. He stared at the man from MI6. 'I saw he'd been beaten—'

'Other marks on his hands, feet, and in the genital area would suggest he underwent considerable pain before he was despatched. A knife across the throat. Was a knife the weapon of choice of your Mr Fisher, DCI Spate?'

Stubbornly, Charlie insisted, 'I still think we should be concentrating on Fisher.'

Cryer interrupted him with a weary, dismissive wave of his hand. 'Perhaps DCI Spate is right. Maybe we should set him loose, seek out the man he believes killed Thomas. The reality is, I don't want an officer on my team who is less than committed to the task I have in hand. That task is to locate and ·capture a terrorist — Ismail Badur. I don't want to be stumbling over DCI Spate's feet while I'm at it.'

Hotly, Charlie snarled, 'I suppose you'll try to put the blame for last night's fiasco on me, or one of our team!'

Cryer regarded him calmly. He shook his head, the kind of gentle admonishment one would give to a child. 'No. The blame — if that's the word for it — lies on no one. The intelligence we received was accurate, as far as it went. We suspect that Ismail Badur did not turn up at the scheduled meeting at Venture Point because plans were changed at the last moment. Something else called him away, distracted him. But no matter . . . that's my business.' He turned to Assistant Chief Constable Charteris. 'I think it best that DCI Spate is released from his attachment to this operation. He's free to be utilised on other enquiries, as far as I'm concerned. At least we'll be spared the danger of blundering into each other with the possible result of endangered operations . . .'

* * *

In Eric Ward's office, Charlie Spate was still burning at the dismissiveness in Major Cryer's remarks, but at least he had got what he wanted. Cryer was chasing shadows. Spate had a quarry in sight . . . and intended getting his hands on him.

'So are you still acting for Joe Fisher?' Spate asked.

Eric Ward held his glance levelly. 'What do you mean?'

'You acted for him over those charges we brought. You got him set loose on the streets. I'm just asking you straight. Is Fisher your client?'

Carefully, Eric replied, 'Joe Fisher has not asked me to act for him since he was released earlier.'

He had the impression DCI Spate didn't believe him. He could feel the resentment still in the policeman: he knew Charlie Spate wanted to believe he was lying. But it was true — Fisher hadn't asked him to represent him. Eric was doing this for Susie Cartwright. 'So you're still after Fisher for the robbery at Delamere.'

'Robbery and *killing*,' Spate asserted. 'Don't forget the old man died, and we can place Fisher at the scene. But that's not the only thing we want him for now. He's in big trouble, your little friend.'

'He's not a friend,' Eric replied quietly.

'Friend, mate, client, call him what you will. He's a scumbag, you let him out on the streets and now people are paying for it,' Spate snapped hotly.

'It was the failure of your people to present the case properly that released Fisher,' Eric contended in a calm tone. 'You're going over old ground and—'

'Old ground it may be, Ward, but there's two people dead as a result of that bastard wandering around out there!'

'Two?'

Spate glared at Eric and nodded. 'You say you saw signs of the activity in South Shields last night.'

'You think Fisher was involved in that?'

Spate managed a thin, cynical smile. 'Didn't I make it clear earlier? I should have let you have the good news straight away. You let Fisher out on the streets, and he gets right back into bed with his other mates to get into the hell knows what, and one of them straight away ends up dead.'

'Who are you talking about?'

'A man called Jag Thomas. He's the low-life character we pulled out of the river last night.' DCI Spate crossed his arms in satisfaction. 'You want to know what I think happened?'

'I've no doubt you're going to tell me.'

'You deserve to know. After all, you allowed it all to be set up.' Spate shook his head. 'The trouble is with these scum — and I've seen it all before — once they get their hands on stuff greed kicks in, they can't agree, nerves snap and big trouble starts. You want to know what I reckon happened?'

Eric was not sure he did, but remained silent.

'I think Fisher pulled that job at Delamere with one other man. It may or may not have been his mate Thomas. It probably was, because although Thomas normally sets things up, doesn't get too closely involved in the heavy stuff himself, I think the prospects of good pickings at the Hall led him to go along with his protégé Fisher. But things didn't fall out as they should have done. They got disturbed; the colonel broke in on them; one of them slammed him on the skull and bingo! Big trouble ahead!'

'This is all theory.'

'Theory, supposition, call it what you like,' Spate sneered, 'but I'm prepared to place my chips on the one hand of cards: they got out of there, the two of them, with loot they didn't agree about. Something on that list you let me have was worth a bundle and they couldn't agree about the split, or the fencing of it, or whatever. Like I told you, I've seen it all before: thieves do fall out. And it all came to a head last night.'

'You think Fisher killed Thomas in a quarrel over the proceeds of the burglary.'

'That'll do nicely for me.'

'You've no direct evidence of all this.'

Charlie Spate shrugged. 'We got DNA that places Fisher at Delamere; we know Fisher and Thomas were mates; the colonel's dead and now so is Thomas, down near where he and Fisher hung out. Whether my scenario is the right one or not, we sure as hell have enough to pull Fisher in, and get his side of the story.'

There was a short silence. At last Eric said quietly, 'I don't know why you came to me with this business.'

'I'll tell you why, Ward. I don't like you. I don't like the clients you handle. And you got Fisher back onto the street when we had him dead to rights. And somehow, you don't ring true to me. You're an ex-copper, and you've crossed over but it's not just that: it's the fact you seem to take pleasure in whacking your ex-colleagues like you did over the Fisher business.'

'That's not true,' Eric replied, maintaining his calm tone in spite of the anger rising in his chest. 'It was just the incompetence of your people and—'

'The hell with it,' Charlie Spate interrupted him, rising from his seat. 'I don't give a damn anyway. I just thought I'd call around here to give you the good news, ask you straight if Fisher was still your client, and . . . warn you.'

'Warn me?' Eric replied coldly.

Spate nodded, placed his knuckles on Eric's desk, leant forward and glared at him. 'Too bloody right! You tell me Fisher isn't on your client list, and I got to take that as the truth. Make it stay that way, Ward. Keep your nose out of our business, or I'll make sure it gets good and bloodied!'

The two men stayed that way for several seconds, both breathing hard, each refusing to look away. At last, with a disgusted grunt, Charlie Spate stood up, moved away from the desk, and grimaced. 'That'll do for now,' he ground out. 'But you hear what I said.' He headed for the door, an insolent swagger in his step. 'So . . . see you in court some time, Mr Ward!'

After Spate had gone Eric sat seething in his chair. He had told Spate the truth, but he had been somewhat less than truthful at the same time. He regretted that: he had involved himself in the case, and maybe he should have admitted it to Spate, but the man got under his skin, irritated him, chafed at him like a raw spot. He drummed his fingers on the desk. He hated stepping back from all this, simply because a man like Spate had threatened him.

There was a light tap on the door. Susie looked in. 'Mr Spate seemed pleased with himself, when he went out.'

'He enjoys throwing his weight around. He just tried it.'

Susie stood in the doorway, hesitantly. 'You must think me a hypocrite, Mr Ward.'

'Why would I think that?'

'I've been criticising your choice of clients for some time.'

'Maybe you're right, Susie, you and Anne,' he admitted wearily. 'Still, now we've got all this work from the Foreign Office . . .'

'I suppose so,' she said hesitantly. 'But now, I'm afraid . . .'

Something cold touched Eric's stomach. He frowned, staring at Susie. 'What's the problem?'

'It's my sister.' Susie's features were sombre. 'She rang me. She wanted to see you. Said she had nowhere else to turn.

So, I'm sorry, but I said I'd fix for her to see you. I hope you don't—'

There seemed to be no way he could escape all this. And the tenor of his meeting with Spate still rankled. Eric set his jaw. 'Susie, don't worry about it. Is she here now?' His secretary nodded, somewhat shamefacedly. 'Bring her in.'

Joe Fisher's mother was Susie Cartwright's older sister but as far as Eric could see there was no physical resemblance between them at all. Mrs Fisher was in her early fifties. She was small, lean, dark-skinned with straight black hair that carried some streaks of grey. Her hair was untidily dressed and so was her skinny body: she gave the impression she cared little for appearances. She wore stained jeans and a worn denim jacket, and her fingers were stained with nicotine. He guessed she chain-smoked: it would account in part for her edginess now, sitting in his office. She'd be nervous, but she probably needed the support of nicotine. Or maybe something else. He cast a glance at Susie, who was hesitating at the door. He nodded to her, reassuringly, and she managed a tight little smile. 'I'll leave you to it, then.'

She closed the door quietly behind her. It was better that she was as little involved in this as possible. Eric recalled Charlie Spate's closing words. He still burnt over the threat. He knew he was being unwise, but this was Susie's sister, and no one was going to tell him what cases he could or could not take.

'All right, Mrs Fisher,' he said quietly. 'What can I do for you?'

She hesitated, fingers twitching in her lap as she sat straight-backed in the chair facing him. 'Thanks for seeing me, Mr Ward. You acted for Joe the last time.'

Eric nodded. 'I hear he's in trouble again.'

She shook her head in grim desperation. 'I been warning him for years, but he never took no notice of me. He had too much of his damned father in him: cocky, swagger, always knew what was best, you know what I mean? He's been in so many scrapes . . . and when you got him off last time I

157

warned him, told him . . . because Susie told me how lucky he was to get off. And it was you who did it, Mr Ward. It's why I come to you now. I'm at my wit's end.'

'I think I should tell you, Mrs Fisher,' Eric said carefully, 'that as far as I can gather, Joe's in pretty bad trouble this time.'

She gave a slight hissing sound and shook her head. Her dark hair fell lank across her eyes and she brushed away a lock impatiently. 'He told me he didn't do it.'

'Do what?' Eric asked.

'Clobber the old man.'

'You mean Colonel Delamere?'

She nodded vigorously. 'He admitted to me he'd been up at Delamere Hall. They'd sussed it out: they reckoned that there'd be a good haul of stuff there, because the old man had a collection of valuables. Jag Thomas, he had a connection you see, in one of the auction houses, and the colonel had sold a few pieces a few months back, and this auction feller did some valuations, and he passed the information on to Jag Thomas — I tell you, I been telling Joe for years to stay away from that Thomas. He was a bad lot.' She clenched her fist. 'But Joe wouldn't listen to me.'

'You know Thomas is dead?' Eric asked.

She raised her head. Her eyes were shadowed; he detected fear in them. 'I heard.'

'The police think Joe might have been involved. They know he was at Delamere Hall the night the colonel was killed. They think he was involved with that killing. Was it Thomas who was with him that night?'

'Joe wouldn't say. Said it would be grassing a mate.'

'Well, it's worse now because the police also think that Joe had a hand in the death of Thomas. He's in bad trouble, Mrs Fisher.'

'Don't I know it?' she wailed. 'He's a bad lot, Mr Ward, I know that, and I shouldn't give him house room, but he's my son and I got to believe him when he says it wasn't him who battered the old man, and he says as well that he had nothing to do with Jag's death. He admits he was with Thomas that night; they were down at the club together, and they had a few drinks, but he says that he and Jag split up about six that evening. But he went back to see Jag later, and he saw something that scared the hell out of him. He wouldn't tell me what he saw but it made him run. And then this woman rang him, and he got really scared—'

'Calm down, Mrs Fisher. Look, there's not really much I can do to help unless Joe turns himself in. If he gives himself up, I . . .' Eric hesitated. Something she had just said worried him, a fluttering in his mind. He dismissed it, irritably. He leant forward, then nodded. 'If what he says is true about Colonel Delamere I'll represent him, do what I can to help, but I have to warn you that it looks as though he's in great difficulty. I'll have to see him, of course.'

'That's it, Mr Ward,' she said eagerly. 'He wants to give himself up. But he's scared.'

'If he comes in,' Eric assured her, 'the police won't do anything other than question him, and I'll be able to sit in on the interview—'

'It's not the police he's scared of, Mr Ward. That's the point! It's what he saw down at Tyne Dock. He's hiding, and he's scared and confused, and he says there's only one person he's got confidence in. That's you, Mr Ward. He wants to meet you, talk to you, get your advice. And then, well, acting on your words he'll give himself up.'

Eric was silent for a little while. 'I'll do what I can, Mrs Fisher, and I'll talk to him. It's best if he comes here to my office—'

'He won't do that, Mr Ward. He's like a scared rabbit. He's been on the phone to me. He wants you to go meet him.'

'Where?'

'He won't say, not straight off.' Mrs Fisher frowned. 'He was on to me and I never heard him like this before. He's in a right panic. Says there's people after him, and after what he saw done to Jag Thomas—'

'Well how am I supposed to meet him if he won't say where?'

Mrs Fisher avoided his eye, twisted her fingers together. 'I hope you won't take this wrong, Mr Ward. He says he'll give you a place, and when you get there he'll phone you, let you know where to go from there.'

'What on earth is the point—'

'It's because he thinks you might get followed,' she burst out, interrupting him as the panic rose in her tones. 'I tell you, he's a bag of nerves. He says to meet you up on the moors, and then he'll phone you once he's sure there's no one following you.'

Eric shook his head doubtfully. 'I see no reason why anyone should be following me.'

'Please, Mr Ward. Otherwise he won't give himself up.' Eric sighed. Susie would be waiting nervously in the outer office. He could not let her down. And DCI Charlie Spate could go to hell. He nodded. 'All right, Mrs Fisher. Give me the time and place and I'll meet him.'

CHAPTER 5

Eric left Susie at the office at six o'clock. She was worried, and showed it: her concern now seemed to be more for Eric than for her sister. It was as though she feared she had imposed a dangerous burden upon him. Eric had said nothing to her about the reason for Spate's visit, of course, and he did not regard his agreement to meet Fisher as carrying any danger for himself. It was a matter of meeting the young man — who was displaying a paranoid regard for his own security, it seemed to Eric — and persuading him to return to Newcastle to give himself up to the police.

The sun was dropping low in the sky as he drove north. The road was a quiet one, surging and swooping across a repeated rhythm of rocky outcrops, a crumpled landscape in which Eric saw shadowy ghosts of villages and furrowed fields of old, isolated churches in a bare landscape, the occasional large farmstead huddled behind a shelter-belt of tall trees that screened the inhabitants from the north-easterly winds that could come scouring over these hills in winter. In the distance there were the military ranges, conifer plantations that would march most of the way up to Carter Bar and the Scottish Border. The roadside symbol of the curlew had long since told him he had entered the Northumberland National

Park: Eric was left with the wry thought that this kind of scenery was a far cry from the usual stamping grounds frequented by Joe Fisher and his kind.

But Fisher had chosen well for his own purposes.

Oddly enough, Eric still felt the odd prickling sensation that he had been experiencing recently, the curious feeling that he was being watched, observed, followed, but the countryside through which he now drove would have made it impossible for anyone to follow him closely: the road was too lonely and ill-frequented, the long views too distant, and somewhere up in these hills Joe Fisher waited, and watched.

'Joe wants you to drive up beyond Simonside,' Mrs Fisher had explained. 'He says he wants you to go up near Deadwater Fell; when you get there he'll phone you, and when he's certain that you're alone, with no one following you, he'll make the arrangements to meet. He's already got your mobile phone number.' She hesitated, shame-faced. 'He had it when you were acting for him before.'

'This all seems over the top,' Eric had muttered.

'It's just that he's really scared,' Mrs Fisher had repeated. 'He's convinced that they're out to get him, the way they got Jag Thomas.'

'And just who are they?' Eric demanded.

She had shaken her head mournfully. 'He doesn't really seem to know. But he's keeping low until you get to him . . . Then he'll talk with you, come in with you, if you think that's best.'

So Eric now found himself in country he loved, the hills where he and Anne had begun their marriage. As he drove he recalled the bracken-strewn lower slopes where they had walked in autumn, the way the birches along the river banks had glowed in a harmony of silver and gold. He remembered how the hills changed, in subtleties of colour, of light and shade, and he recalled the scents of flowers and fungus and earth after a shower of rain. But in those days life had been settled, certain, and he and Anne had walked the sandstone tracks and the crisp smooth turf with deep-seated contentment.

A mission like this was a different affair. He felt tense, scanning the hills about him as he breasted each rise, crossing the brown burns and climbing up towards Deadwater Fell with one eye open for the presence of the frightened young villain he was scheduled to meet. One thing was for certain: he was not followed. Occasionally he caught the glint of late evening sunshine on the windscreen of a car, on a distant summit, on a road leading to the coast, but he met very few cars passing him, and on only two occasions had he pulled in to allow someone to overtake: on each occasion he was convinced the driver had been a farmer, heading for town, Wooler, or Kirknewton, or Rothbury itself.

The final stretches of road to Deadwater Fell petered out into little more than a track, and Eric drove the Celica carefully over the rutted ground. Fisher had not said he should climb up to the fell top itself, merely to make for it.

He knew Fisher had chosen well. There were at least three summits nearby from which a man stationed with field glasses would be able to see — and not be seen. Moreover, since Eric was out in the open on the fellside, the watcher would be able to determine easily whether he was alone or not. With that thought, when he was still some distance from the summit and concerned about the car suspension, Eric pulled in to the side of the track and cut the engine.

Peat and heather abounded around him. In the distance, way below him to his left, he caught a glimpse of the river, glinting in the late sunshine. Miniature versions of the Simonside escarpment lay to his right, small outcroppings and low crags, sharp descents of north-facing sandstone and on the far hill, well-farmed sweet pastures that indicated the presence of limestone. The silence swept in about him. Above him he saw the long, slow sweeping flight of a buzzard, searching for prey. Out on these hills was a man who also saw himself as prey — to some unknown hunter. Eric shook his head doubtfully, not knowing what to make of the whole affair.

Colonel Delamere dead; Jag Thomas following him. And for what? Maybe he would find out when he spoke to Joe Fisher, but he had his doubts about that. From what he had gathered from Mrs Fisher, her son was on the run from someone who had not revealed his identity, and had murder in mind.

Arising out of a burglary at Delamere Hall that had gone badly wrong.

As he sat there with the shadows lengthening about him the thought of Neil Scanlon suddenly drifted into Eric's mind. He had no doubt himself that the investigation the man was carrying out into the deaths of Richard Bethell and Lord Westbury would inevitably be doomed to failure, in the sense that a solution would never be found. Eighty odd years was a long time: the bones of the business would have been picked over many times. It was just food for a conspiracy theorist.

The interest Sarah Castle had shown in Neil Scanlon's theorising had been surprising to Eric — or had it really been interest? Perhaps she was simply being polite that evening in the Greek restaurant. But that was only one thing that intrigued him about Sarah. He found it difficult to work her out. The clear interest she had shown in him at Delamere Hall had been followed by silence; it was she who had then taken the initiative in meeting; and, he was forced to admit, it was she who had taken the initiative at his apartment . . . He half closed his eyes and he could almost remember the lightness of her fingers upon his body, the warm, sensual, practised way in which she had made love, the slow, languorous manner in which she had led him — and her — to a wild, passionate climax.

And since then, again, silence.

His thoughts were still upon her, the way she looked as she lay naked beside him in the dimly lit room, the soft touch of her flesh, when the harsh jangle of his mobile phone brought him back to reality with a start.

'Fisher?'

'It's me, Mr Ward. You come alone?'

'That's the way you wanted it,' Eric said, nettled. 'Where the hell are you?'

* * *

'I can see you, Mr Ward. I been watching . . .' There was a short silence. The young man seemed edgy, uncertain, and his breathing was harsh, excited, as though he had been running. 'You wasn't followed, was you?'

'If you can see me on this God-forsaken fell ridge, you'll know I've not been followed. There's not a soul in sight. Look, Fisher, I've played this game because your mother asked me to, but it's time games were over. Where are we going to meet? And why the hell do you want to meet me anyway?'

'I don't know what's going on, Mr Ward,' the man replied, jerkily. 'We done that burglary, me and Jag Thomas, though he didn't usually do stuff like that himself. Said he'd had a good tip. And it wasn't me who done for the old man. I'd smashed the glass case, and that's when the colonel came chargin' in from the corridor, swingin' his stick. It wasn't me that clobbered him, it was Jag. And anyways, it was an accident, like, really. Jag didn't mean to kill him. But I guess he was an old man and now . . .'

His voice died away, uncertainly. 'Get on with it,' Eric demanded. 'We can talk about all this when we meet. Where—'

'But I want you to understand, Mr Ward. I don't know what the hell's goin' on. We grabbed what we could after the old man went down, and after that everythin' seemed to go wrong. We got this place, see, where Jag stashed stuff he was waiting to fence, and we was just waiting for some of the heat to die down before we got onto something else. And I was back at Tyne Dock, workin' the car ferries again, but things were going all to hell. I had to see someone in the club, and then I went back to meet Jag, and I walked in on them and I saw what that guy was doin' to Jag, and I tell you, Mr Ward, I got out of there fast as I could. And that phone call, it was that what spooked the hell out of me as well. They wanted the statuette—'

'The Anubis statuette?' Eric asked.

'I don't know about that. But it's been nothin' but bad luck since we laid hands on the colonel's stuff. And how did they get my phone number? It spooked me. And there was this guy, I'm sure he was followin' me. And after Jag . . . Look, Mr Ward, I'm scared to hell. I don't want to end up like Jag Thomas.'

'Then you have to come in with me,' Eric urged.

'I know that, but I got to be certain they aren't on your tail. You got to meet up with me. There's this place where Jag and me used to stash the stuff. It'll take you about an hour to get there. I'll meet you there. We got to talk . . . and then, if you give me the protection I need, I'll do as you say. I'll come in with you. But goin' in alone, that's not an option . . . These guys, they'll nail me to the wall, I know it. And in my position, I don't trust the polis. For all I know they could be in on it.'

Men like Joe Fisher would never have great confidence in the police, Eric recognised. 'All right, Joe, tell me. Where do we meet?'

* * *

Two thousand years ago Linshield Furse had been used by the Romans as a fishing port: remains of a wooden jetty had been discovered there three decades ago, the land about had been picked and pored over by archaeologists and then, eventually, everyone had left it in peace to return to the slumberous state it had enjoyed previously, the small harbour silted up, the tall grasses flourishing in the marshy soil, the sandy cove running shallow to the sea some two miles away. There was nothing there now, except for a scattering of cottages in the narrow street that meandered down to what had once been the harbour: most of them were decayed, roofs fallen in, walls crumbling under the invasive attacks of ivy and birch trees, flourishing where fishing folk had once lived and worked.

Three of the cottages had been renovated some fifteen years ago but were rarely used: their owners had used them as holiday cottages expecting a development that had never materialised, largely because the road access was so poor. Someone seemed to be in residence in the top cottage at the moment, for there was a car parked outside the rickety gate. There would be a time, Eric guessed, when an enterprising developer from Newcastle would see potential in this ancient port where none other had, and take the whole renovation programme in hand, but no such entrepreneur had so far appeared. Eric had been told by Fisher it would take him an hour to drive to the deserted village. It had, in fact, been closer to two, partly because of his being delayed by farm tractors on two occasions, in narrow lanes leading down from the moor, partly because he had twice got lost in the meandering tracks, and lastly because of the condition of the road in the last two miles.

Now he waited, watching for signs of the man he was supposed to meet.

Fisher had said that Jag Thomas had had a place where he stashed the products of his nefarious activities, before he fenced them. It was likely to be the long, low-roofed, hangar-like building that had once served as a barn for the former farmhouse adjoining. The farmhouse, like most of the rest of the small village, was in a considerable state of decay, unroofed, its walls twisted with ivy. But the barnlike building attached to it seemed relatively sound in construction.

When he had arrived at the village, Eric had been uncertain what to do: whether to explore, or wait for Joe Fisher to show up. He had finally chosen the latter course, staying in the car, waiting in the gathering darkness. There was no sign of activity, no car, no sounds of movement, no lights. Eric waited, and cursed under his breath at Fisher's melodramatic behaviour.

From time to time he thought he caught the sound of distant cars: the main highway lay some half-mile away, though the track that twisted and meandered its way down to the ancient sea village was much further to traverse. He had seen two vehicles parked up there also, but assumed they belonged to locals who would be out fishing on the point, beyond the sand dunes that had built up over the centuries, barring the way to the sea and killing off the only industry the tiny village had known. But now, as he waited, Eric grew ever more impatient. He checked his watch. It had taken him two hours to reach the village; he had been waiting forty minutes already, and the darkness was growing about him, a thin sliver of moon giving little light to the shadowy, crumbling street at his back. He decided he had waited long enough. It was time to explore, check whether the frightened young thug was still hiding, and if there was no sign of him, it would be time to call the whole thing off. It would be rough on Mrs Fisher, and Susie too for that matter, but Eric was already beginning to regret that he had agreed to enter upon this wild goose chase.

DCI Charlie Spate had warned him to stay clear of Joe Fisher. Eric was now beginning to think he should have taken that piece of advice.

He got out of the car and stretched. He reached inside the glove compartment and took out the flashlight he usually carried there; he cursed when he attempted to switch it on. The battery was dead. He looked about him, uncertain, then decided he might as well take a look at the only place that looked to be a likely building for Jag Thomas to have used — the only construction of any size in the village that seemed to be in a decent state of repair. He made his way towards the old barn, attached to the crumbling farmhouse. Briefly, his way was illuminated by the moonlight: a faint shadow preceded him, but as he neared the barn itself it faded, light streaks of cloud darkening the sky once more.

He reached the entrance which lay to one side: a wooden door, it appeared to be in good condition. It was unlocked, and as he put his hand to it the door swung open slightly.

There was no screech of rusty hinges. The door was well oiled. Eric hesitated, then decided to investigate further rather than go into the barn. He followed the wall along its length. A second door lay at the rear of the building: he did not try it, but walked past until he entered a yard.

There was a car parked there.

Eric cursed. It would be Fisher's. The young thug would be inside the barn, cowering no doubt, waiting to see whether the arrival was the man who had agreed to help him, or one of the demons of his fantasies, men who were out to kill him. Angrily, Eric walked back towards the first door. He put his hand to it, pushed it open. 'Fisher? Where the hell are you?'

The interior of the barn was in darkness. Eric hesitated, angry with himself for not having a torch to hand. He called out again. 'Fisher? It's Eric Ward. For God's sake stop cowering in there. You said we should meet here. Now where the hell are you?'

He had stepped forward, two paces into the barn, and the ground beneath his feet felt earthy, and he smelt dampness. A hell of a place to store stolen goods, he thought to himself. Then he became aware of something else. It was the whisper of a movement, a slight swishing sound, someone sliding along the wall in the darkness and he began to turn, back away towards the door, but the slight noise was behind him, he felt a hand briefly touch his shoulder and then something hit him, hard, just behind the ear. He staggered, lurched to one side as a second blow took him on the side of the head. His senses swimming, Eric fell to his knees as lights exploded in his skull. He was vaguely aware of the soft, churned earth under his knees and then he was falling forward as all sense and feeling deserted him, the yawning pit of blackness opened up to devour him, and then there was only the void.

* * *

The light hurt his eyes. It sent jagged lances of pain into his brain. When he tried to focus, all he could make out was a dim form, some feet away from him. It was a man in a tattered shirt, kneeling, head down. A strange, choking sound came to him. The man was crying, sobbing, gasping for breath.

Senses reeling from the vicious blow to the back of his head, Eric tried to bring order to his mind. He was aware that he was lying on his side. When he tried to move, sit up, he realised his hands were pinioned behind his back. He twisted his hands, and a sharp pain shot through his wrists. Wire. The thin wire that bound him was cutting into his wrists. There was a slickness on his hands: his own blood.

He rolled, began to rise. The man across the room from him was imprisoned in a narrow pool of light. When he focused, Eric realised that, incongruously, the illumination came from an art deco lamp, its tight-breasted, naked female figure reaching up, holding the shade that was tilted towards the man's head. For several seconds Eric stared at the man; then he recognised him.

It was Joe Fisher.

He was crying. He was on his knees crying, sobbing, uncontrolled sounds that carried the tone of desperation and terror. He too seemed to be bound, arms locked behind his back. Then Eric noted with horror that Fisher's left ear had been sliced away, and was hanging from a sliver of cartilage. There was blood collecting around his knees, also, a slow, dark congealing on the earthen floor of the barn.

Eric looked about him wildly. The pool of light was concentrated on Joe Fisher: behind him stretched the vault of the barn, dark and empty. Evidence of its former use was faintly revealed in the dimness: some projecting, broken-slatted walls that would have been erected to serve as byres in long gone days. And this was the place that Jag Thomas and Fisher had used as a temporary store for goods they had acquired in burglary. The art deco lamp probably: irrelevantly, Eric wondered where it might have been stolen from. He tried to say something, croak Joe Fisher's name, but as he did so he heard movement, someone approaching. A hand took him by the shoulder, pulled him upwards, forcing him into the position held by Joe Fisher. On his knees, hands bound behind his back, Eric looked up at the man who had attacked him in the darkness.

He was perhaps late thirties; his face was strong, handsome even, his nose prominent, beaked. He wore a beard, dark in colour, of perhaps two or three weeks' growth. His hair was matted, black, tight in its curling thick mass. He squatted in front of Eric, inspecting his features closely, with an alert curiosity. He was silent for a while. Eric felt contempt in his glance. Then he spoke. 'My name is Ismail Badur, although I have used many others.' His English was accurate, his accent pronounced. Eric could not place it, other than to believe it to be Middle Eastern. 'You will perhaps have heard of me. Ismail Badur. Who are you?'

Eric struggled to find his voice. It came out as a harsh croak. 'I came here looking for Fisher.'

'I did not ask why you come. I asked you for your identity.' The man stood up suddenly, towering over Eric. He placed his hands on his hips and kicked Eric on the thigh with his left foot as though emphasising a point. 'I ask again. Who are you?'

'I'm his lawyer,' Eric growled.

'Lawyer.' Ismail Badur grunted. 'All lawyers are liars and fornicators.'

'You'll have to talk to the Law Society about that,' Eric snarled, incensed.

His captor was silent for a few minutes, regarding Eric as though he were some unknown specimen under the microscope. Then he grunted again. 'I think you do not take me seriously.' He half turned, gestured towards Joe Fisher. 'He takes me seriously. Now. You see what I have done with him?'

'I see,' Eric spat out the words.

'I cut him, many places, but still he lies to me. You. The lawyer. You will not lie to me, I think.' Eric's captor paused. His dark eyes seemed intense in their gaze, as the light from the lamp outlined his features. 'Where is the jackal-god?'

For a few moments Eric failed to understand what the man was talking about. Then the realisation dawned, slowly. The Anubis figure. The ebony and gold statuette stolen from Delamere Hall. He looked past Ismail Badur to the sobbing figure of Joe Fisher. He shook his head. 'Is that what all this is about?' He shook his head again, in disbelief. 'I've no idea.'

There was a long silence. The man standing in front of him appeared to be contemplating something. At last he lowered his hands from his hips, nodded towards the sobbing Joe Fisher. 'The boy says he does not have it. *You* say you do not have it. I think you lie. And we waste time. I could cut you, like him . . .'

The man's fingers curled, but he seemed uncertain about something. He hesitated, then suddenly turned and walked away from the pool of light, made his way into what seemed to be a small room to the right. Eric heard him scuffling there, dragging something. He looked at Fisher; the young man's head was low now, his forehead almost touching the floor. His sobs were stifled, ragged. As Ismail Badur continued to pull something from the room to the right Eric heard another sound, a slight scuffling movement, a rat in the darkness beyond the byres, attracted perhaps by the scent of blood, dripping from Joe Fisher, spreading a dark stain about his knees.

Ismail Badur came out of the side room, and shuffled towards them. Eric turned his head: he could see now what the man was dragging. It was a heavy, inert body. The corpse was dragged towards the pool of light, then dropped unceremoniously between the two kneeling captives. Joe Fisher did not raise his head; he was sinking lower, snivelling softly. As Eric watched, Ismail Badur wound his fingers in the collar of the black leather jacket, twisting it so that the dead man's face came into Eric's line of sight. The man's eyes were wide, as though startled. There was something familiar about him, something that jogged Eric's memory, the short, cropped hair, the muscular shoulders . . .

The Steamboat. Eric had seen him before, but only briefly, the night Jackie Parton had taken him to the south bank of the Tyne to meet Philly Fredericks. He had come into the bar, drained a glass of whisky, gone out again into the night.

'You see what I did to this man!' Ismail Badur asked in a threatening tone. 'It is time you take me as a man of my word.'

The dead man's throat had been gashed wide open. His lifeblood had drained away there, in the darkness.

'It is what also I did to the man Thomas, down at the riverside.' Ismail Badur jerked his head, glanced around. 'It was he who squealed like a pig when he told me about this place, told me that this is where I would find this boy — this *client* of yours.'

He released his grip on the dead man's collar, and the body slumped to the ground. Ismail Badur stared at it for a moment then nodded, reflecting. 'This man was not like Thomas. This man, he came looking for me. But I met him in the darkness. He was a good fighter. A trained man. But he is dead. And I live.' The dark eyes turned back to Eric. 'You . . . you are not a trained man. You are a lawyer. A man of secrets and lies. You, it will be easy to kill. But that will not bring me the jackal-god.' He paused, glanced at Joe Fisher. 'This boy, he says he does not have it. But he calls his lawyer to his side. So . . . he is your client. Lawyers are liars and fornicators, but they have a twisted loyalty to their clients, do they not!'

He stepped away, back into the pool of light from the art deco lamp. He reached behind him, took from his belt a thin-bladed knife. 'You will tell me now where I will find the jackal-god.'

'I don't know where it is,' Eric insisted.

Ismail Badur held the knife in his right hand. He moved towards Joe Fisher, took up a stance behind him, then leant forward and wound the fingers of his left hand into Fisher's long hair. Slowly, carefully, almost gently he lifted the young man's head, exposing the vulnerable neck. Fisher's eyes were rolling in his head, almost sightless. His mouth gaped open, slavering, as Ismail Badur forced the head back, exposing further the naked throat.

'I told you I killed the man Thomas. You have seen what I did to the man lying there,' Ismail Badur whispered. 'This man is your client. Save him, lawyer, *save* him!' Desperately, Eric tried to rise from his knees. 'I'm telling you the truth! I don't know what's happened to the Anubis statuette! It'll do you no good—'

'He is your client, lawyer! You are the keeper of his secrets. He calls to you and you come.' Ismail Badur snarled, pressing the knife blade to Joe Fisher's throat. '*Save him!*'

Rigid, Eric stared at the assassin, knowing it was hopeless.

He could not prevent this nightmare happening. He saw the wild, staring determination in the killer's eyes, knew that the man would have no compunction whatsoever in slicing the life from Joe Fisher, knew there was nothing he could do to save the boy.

Then something moved in the dark barn; at the corner of his eye he caught sight of a movement near the byres. It escaped Ismail Badur: he concentrated his gaze on Eric, held the knife close against Joe Fisher's throat.

'Stop! Stop it right there!'

Ismail Badur must have been startled, but he gave no sign of surprise. He stayed exactly as he was, fingers wound in Joe Fisher's hair, the knife blade pressing against the jugular vein. Eric turned his head to the dark figure that had emerged from the side of the byre. The sound he had heard when Ismail Badur was preoccupied, dragging out the body of his last victim, had been not a rat, but someone who had entered the barn from the back entrance Eric had noted earlier. He stared, and realised it was a woman.

Moreover, after a moment he realised he knew her. 'Sarah!' he gasped.

And yet it was not like Sarah at all. Her hair was tightly drawn back from her face. She was wearing a dark jacket, jeans, trainers. She was standing behind Ismail Badur with her legs wide apart, on the balls of her feet, knees bent, half-crouching as she stared intently at the man holding Joe Fisher. Her arms were extended, steady, levelled, both hands clasping the pistol aimed at the back of Ismail Badur's head. It was a rigid, controlled, menacing stance.

'Stop now. Drop the knife.' Her voice echoed harshly in the dark barn. She spoke again, in what might have been Arabic. Then she reverted once more to English. 'Drop the knife, you bastard, or I'll blow off the back of your head, and send you straight to hell!'

Ismail Badur made no move. He made no attempt to look behind him, or seek any way out of his situation. It was almost as though he had not heard her. He was staring almost vacantly at Eric, dreamily, and a slow smile touched his beaded lips. In a quiet, determined voice, he said, 'Not hell, *inshallah*. I seek the Promised Garden.'

It was over in a moment. A moment's hesitation, and then he swept the sharp-bladed knife across Joe Fisher's throat in one swift, fierce stroke. A split second later his features disintegrated, blood, bone and brain matter flew about Eric as the snap of the gunshot reverberated in the echoing barn.

Joe Fisher's life gurgled away from him. Ismail Badur was lying across Fisher, sprawled, inert, his face a ruin.

Sarah Castle was kneeling beside Eric. 'Are you all right?'

She tested his bonds, realised his captor had used wire, hesitated, looked Eric in the eye and then stood up, stepped away, holstered the gun and snapped open a mobile phone. He watched her dumbly as she spoke rapidly into the phone. It was not a language he understood.

He remembered this woman, smiling at him across the restaurant table; he remembered the warm caresses, the passionate movement of her body against his.

Now she was different. She was a professional.

* * *

'How are you, Mr Ward?'
'I'll survive.'

175

'Yes, you seem to have developed a certain talent for survival.'

Linwood-Forster seemed rather pleased with himself. While Eric sat coldly behind his desk the civil servant wandered around the room, running his hand over the back of the chair, reading some of the titles of the law books on the shelves, gazing with a half-smile out of the window towards the sunlit Quayside. 'I understand from the office that the early work on the immigration files we gave you has been quite satisfactory.'

'Things have gone well enough,' Eric replied, rather grumpily.

'Yes, well, I'm pleased we made the correct decision. The work is well-placed.' Linwood-Forster turned, gazed at Eric with a self-satisfied smile. 'However, I thought it would be well if I came in to see you, to talk to you about this other business. As a matter of courtesy. And, I admit, as a necessary precaution. We are your clients, of course, and as we've already agreed, you are bound by the rules of confidentiality. But it is as well to satisfy your curiosity. So you need ask no . . . unwelcome questions later.'

He moved languidly to the chair in front of Eric's desk and seated himself carefully. He brushed his sleeve in the gesture characteristic of his fussy concern with his appearance. 'I must confess that the whole matter could have been handled rather better. At one time it was all rather like a Whitehall farce — people running around in circles chasing each other.'

'Two men died — apart from Colonel Delamere and that thug Thomas,' Eric said coldly. 'I don't see anything funny in that.'

'You are right to admonish me,' Linwood-Forster replied blandly. 'My comparison was not well chosen.'

'But you're here to tell me what the hell was going on.'

'Quite so.' Linwood-Forster nodded thoughtfully. 'The London Conference has now commenced, and while we have no great expectations, we do at least still have hopes . . .'

'The conference on the future of the Middle East?' Eric asked sharply. 'What's that got to do with what's been happening?'

Linwood-Forster scratched at his cheek with a delicate fingernail. 'It was the conference that brought the whole thing to a head, in reality. But perhaps I'd better start at the beginning. With Colonel Delamere. And the letter you sent to us at the Foreign Office.'

'As the colonel's executor.'

'Quite so . . . The colonel had already written to the Foreign Office some months previously. Perhaps you already knew that. Unfortunately, the letter was received by a young man who . . . well, shall we say his loyalties actually lay elsewhere? He never passed the letter to the appropriate level of seniority: instead, he communicated its contents to certain friends of his in the Arab movement, who supported him financially in return for such titbits, and suppressed the letter itself.' He paused, frowning slightly. 'That matter has now been settled, of course. The gentleman concerned has been dealt with . . . discreetly, as one would expect.'

'What did the colonel say in the letter?' Eric asked curiously.

'Oh, we'll come to that in a moment. It was at this point that, quite independently, MI6 became involved. You'll probably be aware that security matters these days are very largely concerned with electronic chatter, I think they call it. Officers in MI6 began to pick up traffic that made them prick up their ears. It was connected with the forthcoming conference in London, when it was hoped — still hoped in fact — that a settlement of outstanding tensions in the Middle East will be achieved. I doubt that myself, with Hamas, and Fatah, and the Israeli government . . .'

He flicked at his sleeve again, thoughtfully. 'We were consulted about the matter, and began our own internal investigation — which led to the removal of the gentleman I've already mentioned — but it was decided by MI6 that no action could be taken immediately, other than surveillance operations, until we knew precisely what was going on. What these people out there, who were getting so excited, were after.'

'Which was?'

'The Anubis statuette.' Linwood-Forster nodded sagely to himself. 'We don't know quite how the jackal-god came into Delamere's possession — we think it was family connections, a niece of the Bethells in the first instance, and then a succession of people . . . Nor do we know exactly when the colonel discovered the secret it contained. And we must remember he was a collector. He would always have been reluctant to give up the artefact. However, when the London Conference was scheduled and the colonel realised how the statuette could be used, his patriotism got the better of him and he decided to inform the Foreign Office of his ownership of the artefact. And of what it contained. To his surprise, he received nothing more than a mere acknowledgment.' Linwood-Forster eyed Eric owlishly. 'The aforementioned mole in the department.'

'But what was so important about the statuette?'

'Patience, dear boy, patience.' Linwood-Forster cleared his throat delicately. 'After what he saw as a rebuff, the colonel shrugged his shoulders over the matter for the moment, but approached you with instructions that in the event of his death another letter would be sent — by you this time — informing us once more of the existence of the statuette. Unfortunately, death came rather sooner than he had expected.' Linwood-Forster frowned. 'It was coming in any case. We knew of the existence of the terrorist cell in South Shields, such an unlikely place, one would think, but with its history . . . and from intercepted transmissions MI6 knew that a certain Ismail Badur—'

'I've met the man,' Eric interrupted grimly.

'Quite so. Ismail Badur would be arriving to take charge of the operation, to recover the statuette. In fact, he was planning to break in at Delamere Hall to do just that when he was forestalled by two petty local villains.'

'Fisher and Thomas.'

'Precisely. And we know what happened there. Thomas killed Delamere, the two men fled with certain artefacts — including the statuette, which curiously was also the murder weapon — and Ismail Badur was frustrated. For a while. But it was not long before he was on the track of the thieves. It would be only a matter of time before he caught them. But time was becoming of the essence. He needed to get the statuette before the London Conference really got under way.'

'But why—'

Linwood-Forster held up a restraining hand. 'Let me explain this in my own way. Logically. Step by step. So much more ordered, don't you agree?' He adjusted his cuffs, and grimaced in satisfaction. 'So, he did indeed find the man Thomas. He beat him badly. Tortured him. Thomas admitted they had taken the statuette but declared it was in the possession of Fisher. It had been taken to their so-called warehouse in Northumberland. Linshield Furse. Interesting name.' He paused, musing. 'Quite an eclectic little collection of valuables they had there, too, I understand . . .' He glanced at Eric, coolly. 'Of course, Ismail Badur didn't know you were also looking for Fisher.'

'And while I was looking for Fisher, this man, the MI6 agent—'

'Major Cryer.'

'He was on the trail of the terrorist.'

'Quite so.'

'But how did Cryer come to be at the warehouse?'

Linwood-Forster shrugged. 'Electronic trails. Once Fisher used his mobile phone to you, Cryer knew where Fisher would go. And he knew also that Ismail Badur was hot on the trail. He tried to get Ismail Badur there, but met more than his match in the darkness. The terrorist killed Cryer . . . such an impulsive man for an experienced field officer, you would have thought he would never have gone alone. A matter of pride, perhaps, wanting to make his name, over-confident in his own abilities . . .'

'So Ismail Badur fought Cryer in the darkness and killed him. He told me that much. But Badur was waiting for Fisher . . . who eventually turned up, after telling me he'd meet me at the warehouse.'

Linwood-Forster nodded. 'To Ismail Badur's fury and disappointment Fisher denied he had the statuette. He claimed to have thrown it away, in fear, after witnessing the terrorist's treatment of Thomas. He had seen some of what went on at Tyne Dock that night . . . Ismail Badur tried to persuade Fisher to admit he still had the jackal-god, but to no avail. He didn't believe Fisher could have thrown it away in panic, and then you walked in . . .'

The room was silent for a little while, as each man dwelt on his own thoughts. At last Eric murmured, 'I suppose he would have murdered me too, when he learnt I couldn't help him. If it hadn't been for Sarah . . .'

'Yes . . . It was she who called us, to tell us of your predicament. She wasn't present when assistance arrived, of course . . .'

Linwood-Forster watched Eric carefully as he struggled to ask the question. 'How did she come to be there? What did she have to do with all this?' Frustrated, he burst out, 'Who exactly is she?'

Linwood-Forster hesitated. He glanced around him. 'While you were in hospital, being treated for concussion, and the injuries to your wrists, we did a sweep in your office here. We found the listening device in your telephone. Your line was bugged, as they say in the trade. We took a look in your car too. There was a tracking device underneath the passenger seat.' He raised an eyebrow. 'We . . . ah . . . also took the liberty of entering your apartment. I'm sure you'll have noticed no disturbance. Our people are really quite efficient in such matters. The phone there also contained an appropriate device. Your movements and conversations have been under surveillance for some time, Mr Ward. Not by us.'

'By Sarah Castle?' Eric asked, amazed.

'Of course.'

He sat there and recalled how she had asked him to drive her back to Jarrow after their lunch. How she had seemed to drop something, her keys, and fumble underneath the seat. Then there was the phone call she had asked to make from his office, while he waited for her in the anteroom . . . time enough to plant a device. And then his apartment . . . when she had left him briefly, lying in the warm darkness, the scent of her body in his nostrils . . .

'Who is she?' he asked dully.

'I believe she commenced her career as a . . . how do they describe such people? A honey trap.' Linwood-Forster's eyes were watchful. 'It's a term used to describe women whose job it is to seduce targets, in order to obtain information from them, or produce embarrassing photographs of a sexual nature for blackmail purposes . . .'

Or to plant listening devices, Eric thought numbly. He could still recall the practised way she had made love . . . 'More recently, of course,' Linwood-Forster explained, 'it would seem she has been . . . promoted to more important tasks.'

'She told me she was a journalist,' Eric protested.

'No. Her journalist story was a false trail. She's a field agent, attached to Felshaw's shipping agency merely to provide her with a cover story.'

'A field agent? You mean she also works for MI6?' Eric asked incredulously.

'Oh, no, not at all.' Linwood-Forster's tone was bland. 'All sorts of people have been interested in hunting down the jackal-god. It seems she works for Israeli Intelligence. Sarah Castle — or to put it more accurately, Sarah Weismann — is employed as a field agent by Mossad.'

Eric sat silently, his mind churning with memories. He realised now that Sarah's first invitation to lunch had been deliberately arranged: she knew Scanlon used that restaurant, and wanted an excuse to be there, find out how much he had discovered about the statuette. It was the reason for the second visit also, when she had been brought up to date with his researches . . .

'As I said earlier,' Linwood-Forster continued. 'It's been almost like a Whitehall farce. You, and that policeman DCI Spate looking for Fisher; MI6 looking for Ismail Badur; Mossad seeking the jackal-god; all stumbling over each other, getting in each other's way.'

'And all because of an ebony statuette,' Eric said slowly. 'But you haven't told me why it's so important.'

Linwood-Forster sighed. 'There's no reason why you should not be told, now. The story begins long ago. An artefact placed in the tomb of the boy-king Tutankhamun. Anubis, the jackal-god, Guardian of the Dead, which three thousand years later was looted from the tomb, by Carter or by Lord Carnarvon, it matters not which. It was Carter, certainly, who discovered its secret. Both he and Carnarvon somewhat indiscreetly mentioned that they had come across papyri in the tomb. Something they later denied.' He smiled, and nodded. 'It was the Italian archaeologist Belzoni, in 1817, who first realised that the pharaohs often stored in their tombs a history and account of their reign. It was the practice to encase the papyri, on which such accounts were written, in an object, by way of protection. Henry Salt found one in the hollowed out kilt of an underworld deity — imagine! And then there was the Amherst Papyrus discovered inside a statuette from the reign of Rameses IX. It detailed the trial of ancient tomb robbers some sixteen hundred years before Christ. Fascinating . . .'

Impatiently, Eric began to speak but Linwood-Forster forestalled him. 'That was the secret of the Anubis statuette, you see: in a secret compartment, it contained a papyrus, an account of the reign of the boy-king. A history of the reign of Tutankhamun . . . Delamere discovered the hidden compartment. He discovered the account — in its original form, perhaps, but if not, probably a translation of it by the philologist friend of Carter's, one Alan Gardner.'

Eric was puzzled. 'An account of the reign of the Pharaoh Tutankhamun . . . Great historical interest to academics, I grant you. But was it worth *killing* for?'

Linwood-Forster eyed him cynically. 'Men die for much lesser causes, Mr Ward. As for this . . . it all started long ago, when the pharaoh of the day forsook the traditional gods, broke away from the polytheism practised for four thousand years and established a new city — Amarna — for the worship of the Sun God. He was called Akhenaton. His descendant, eventually, was Tutankhamun.'

'So?' Eric asked, still puzzled in the pause that followed.

Linwood-Forster sighed. 'Debates have raged — if arguments between dried-up archaeologists and elderly academics can ever be said to *rage* — for decades about the identity of the Pharaoh of the Exodus from Egypt. Some argue it was the great king Rameses who enslaved the Israelites and brought about the alarming events that led to Moses leading the Jews from Egypt. Others contend it was Akhenaton himself who was the Pharaoh of the Exodus. But all was based on conjecture merely; a playing with dates, a translation of hieroglyphs, a carving on a temple wall. Tutankhamun never entered the equation, of course: after all, his very existence could only be guessed at before Carter found his tomb in 1922, since all mention of his reign had been erased from the records of stone by his successor. But what if a papyrus record was found, contemporaneous with the story of the Exodus, in the boy-king's tomb?'

'I still don't see—'

'Carter realised its significance, when he found it. The papyrus linked the life of Moses with the Amarna age. That brought into question the very rudiments of the Biblical story, the Exodus, the conquest of Canaan, so crucial to the foundation of ancient Israel. And, incidentally, the claim to the establishment of a modern Jewish state in Palestine.'

'The account would overthrow the whole basis of the Exodus story,' Eric said slowly.

'Quite. It would locate the travels of the Israelites at a different place, in a different time. And that was the trump card he flourished in the face of a certain Embassy official in Cairo in 1922. Help me get back to the diggings, support me in my demands against the Egyptian government, or I'll expose this story to the world.'

'The British government—'

'The British government would have been mightily embarrassed. They had made much political investment in Egypt, made conflicting promises to Arabs and Jews — and now the Palestine Arabs would have proofs to call into question the historical claim of the Zionists to settle in Palestine. Carter's exposure of the papyrus would have precipitated a severe political crisis. The government had to shut him up. So they caved in to his demands. The story wasn't told, Carter got what he wanted, the statuette and its contents were given to the Bethells for safe keeping . . . and so it went on.'

'The papyrus encased in the jackal-god image,' Eric said slowly, 'identified Tutankhamun as the Pharaoh of the Exodus—'

'Which would have meant Moses led his people out of *Amarna*. Which by logical extension would mean that the story of the Exodus was the muddle of myth and legend that many had always believed it to be . . . and consequently, that the Israelites had no real historic right to the lands they now claimed as their birthright.'

Eric was silent for a little while, thinking things through. Slowly, he shook his head. 'All right, I can accept that this might have caused a storm in 1921, with the British government caught in a cleft stick politically, but are you seriously suggesting that now, in the twenty-first century—'

'Fanaticism does not deal in logical time,' Linwood-Forster asserted seriously. 'And that's what we are dealing with: *fanatics*. Ismail Badur was one such. The London Conference was scheduled. For the first time there is a realistic chance of Hamas, and Fatah, their own government, the Israeli government, all coming together to reach a form of agreement. But what would happen if some bunch of fundamental terrorist fanatics came up with proof that the historical right of the Jews to the land of Israel is based on a falsehood. *Proof,* mind you, not mere conjecture!'

Eric understood. The conference would have been torpedoed. The Arab cause would have been loud in its condemnation. Another dreary, murderous round of conflict over ideology, religion and land would have begun. Ismail Badur had intended to provide the weapon; Major Cryer had been out to prevent that happening; Sarah Castle — or Weismann, he now knew — alerted by her employers to the hunt for the jackal-god was also trying to prevent publication of the papyri.

'Of course,' Linwood-Forster added as though reading his mind, 'it would have been more sensible if the two Intelligence services had pooled resources, Mossad and MI6, working together . . . but when did such services ever trust each other? At least, the threat is now over.'

'The statuette can't be found?'

Linwood-Forster shrugged his lean shoulders. 'The only man who knows what happened to it is dead. He probably discarded it in his panicked flight from the Tyne, up into Northumberland, after seeing what had happened to his colleague Thomas. He knew the statuette was deadly. So he probably got rid of it. Who knows what happened to it? And the conference has started.'

'You still have to take Neil Scanlon into account,' Eric warned.

'Ah, yes, the writer of conspiracies.' Linwood-Forster's thin smile had a contemptuous edge. 'Well, of course, he can write about a secret that was communicated to the Bethells; he can construct fanciful theories about the deaths of Richard Bethell and Lord Westbury; he can sell his books in their thousands. But in the end, other than cranks, who can believe what he has to say? He is known to make a living out of conspiracy theories. What is it all but an entertainment? No . . . I don't think we need concern ourselves too much about Mr Scanlon. Let him write his book; let him enjoy his royalties; let the gullible public be misled along doubtful byways.'

'Even if based on truth.' In spite of himself, Eric asked, 'Do *you* think the Bethells were murdered? Do you think they were killed because they refused to disclose the whereabouts of the ebony statuette of the jackal-god? And if so, who killed them?'

Linwood-Forster stood up. In a grave tone, he said, 'Is my opinion of any worth? Who knows? What I am sure of however is that Mr Scanlon will never find *proof* of the murder of Richard Bethell and Lord Westbury. And the rest is . . . merely conjecture, is it not?'

* * *

With his face crushed in the soft, warm, yielding parenthesis of her breasts, Charlie could hardly breathe. 'I had a fag the other day,' he complained in a muffled tone.

'Post-coital?' she asked.

'What?'

'You know, fag after a shag, it's the standard procedure, I'm told.'

'You watch too many films,' he muttered. 'I had a fag because I'm depressed.'

'You didn't seem too unhappy a few minutes ago.'

'Well, I am,' Charlie insisted. 'And it's not just the fact things haven't gone well over the Fisher business.'

'Everyone else seems to have got there before you,' she agreed.

'Well, yes, but it's not that. The fact is I'm in love with you.'

'And I'm thinking of opening a brothel,' Elaine said calmly.

'What?'

'My mother always said I made great broth,' she explained.

'Will you be serious?' he asked plaintively. 'I'm trying to tell you—'

'Don't. Love is for Hollywood heroes in shoot-em-up soap operas. Not for you and me, Charlie.'

'I don't see—'

She shifted in the bed. He gulped down some cool air. Her face was a dim shape in the darkness. 'Look . . . don't start going down that road, Charlie. We're adults. We work together. You're my boss. We choose what to do in our spare time. Don't complicate things. Tell me you lust for me, by all means. But otherwise—'

'But the fact is I just don't know where I stand with you,' he moaned. 'You blow hot, then cold. I never know whether you're going to be receptive, or whether I'm welcome—'

'Lemme make it clear, then. There's no one I'd rather have bouncing my bed springs than you, Charlie. But it's got to be on my terms. When I say so. Now if you don't like the fact that you're not in control, well, that's your problem. Whenever I'd like you to come around, I'll tell you. But don't expect me to be at your beck and call. They have to be my whims, not yours. If you can't handle that, Charlie, well . . .'

It made sense, what she said. And maybe he'd been over-reacting. Maybe it was just lust, and annoyance that he wasn't calling the shots; maybe not love at all. And the rest of it — the botched business over Fisher, and Ismail Badur, and Cryer . . .

'You still unhappy, Charlie?'

He mumbled uncertainly.

He felt her reaching for him again. 'Let's try this, then. See if it makes a difference.'

It made a difference. The rest of it was just business, anyway. In a little while, Charlie had never felt so happy.

* * *

Three miles away in the apartment in Gosforth, Eric Ward switched on the bedside light, unable to sleep. He thought about the woman who had last slept in this bed. After making that phone call, to get assistance for him, she had left. Disappeared. He knew he'd never see her again.

A ghost. A chimaera. Something . . . someone to forget.

He looked at his watch. It was a stupid time to call. But after a while he reached for the phone.

Sharon Owen took a long time to respond. When she did, her voice was groggy with sleep. 'Who's that?'

'Eric.'

'It's late . . .' He heard rustling sounds as she turned over in bed. 'Hell, I hope you're not ringing about the briefs you sent me. For that matter, what am I doing, working on the bloody things in bed and falling asleep over them anyway? Taking work to bed, for God's sake . . . Eric?'

'Yes.'

'What do you want?'

There was a short silence. At last, Eric took a deep breath as though he was about to dive into the deep end of the swimming pool. 'I've been thinking of going away for the weekend. Next weekend. I know a little country pub, just north of Warkworth.'

'Good for you.'

He hesitated again. 'I wonder whether you'd like to come along with me. For the weekend.'

She was silent. The seconds dragged past. Eric waited. 'Of course,' he muttered at last, 'if you can't make it, or have other things to do . . .'

He heard her yawn. 'Hell's flames, Eric, couldn't you have picked a better time to ask?'

'Well—'

She interrupted him. 'I'd love to join you.' She yawned again. 'Look forward to it, in fact. I thought . . . I thought you'd never get around to asking . . .'

She put the phone down.

Eric lay in the darkness, sleep still eluding him. But at least he was happier. His practice was on the up. He'd come to a decision. He was getting on with his life . . .

* * *

The Flying Spindrift edged out into the main channel leading out to sea. Attached to a bow-line came the ponderous, grey and blue shape of the freighter, laden with luxury cars for the

188

African and Middle East markets. The line aft drooped from the freighter as the second tug, the *Yarm Cross,* released itself from its manoeuvring duties. A siren called, echoing from the banks of the Tyne, the freighter acknowledging the assistance as the open sea beckoned at the mouth of the river.

The passage of the freighter sent relatively minor waves lapping to the shoreline on either side of the river, and when the tugs turned away to head back to the berths, and their next tasks later in the day, it was they who caused the greater disturbance as they fussed their way up river against the tide.

Below them the water was dark, sand and mud swirling under their passage. The heavy piece of ebony with the carved mask was lying on its side in the churning mud, undetected, unseen.

It was a long way from the hot sands where it had first been buried, along with its secret, three thousand years ago. It had been entombed then with the boy-king, Guardian of the Dead, to lie there for eternity, until it had been resurrected, almost a hundred years ago . . . Now it was buried again, in the slow, churning silt of the black water.

Perhaps for another hundred years.

Perhaps, this time, for eternity.

THE END

FREE KINDLE BOOKS

Made in the USA
Columbia, SC
12 February 2021

32816750R00117